IN THE GARDEN OF RUSTING GODS

A COLLECTION

By Patrick Freivald

BARKING DEER PRESS

Cover artwork & design by Dean Samed
Interior artwork by Greg Chapman
Interior design by Michael Bailey

Barking Deer Press

Trade Paperback Edition
ISBN: 978-0-9994495-9-2

"Freivald's range is on full display with *In the Garden of Rusting Gods*. Here lies science, horror, humor, and the weird. Action, panic, and dread. Loaded with energy, you'll be tapping to the beat from page one."– Josh Malerman, *New York Times* Best Selling author of *Bird Box* and *Unbury Carol*

"Smart, funny, intriguing, horrifying; Freivald shows us the wide range of his talents." – Kaaron Warren, Aurealis Award-winning author of *The Grief Hole*

"A haunting collection of beautifully desperate characters creatively mingled in the agony of their realities."
– Kelli Owen, author of *Teeth* and *Wilted Lilies*.

TABLE OF CONTENTS

FROM ROBOTS TO BEES TO BEAUTY

AN INTRODUCTION BY WESTON OCHSE

When I was asked by Patrick to write the introduction for him for his collection In the Garden of Rusting Gods, I wasn't sure how to respond. So, I thought of my first collection which had an intro from Joe Lansdale and went back and read it. I noted that half of the introduction was about the worry he had that he wouldn't like my work (he did). Another part of it was that he thought that maybe he'd written enough introductions to pay back those who had helped him as he became the writer he is today.

In Joe's own words: *This is not because I think I am above it, but due to the fact that I have now been writing and selling for near on forty years, and have been a full time writer for soon to be thirty years, and I'm feeling a little short on time in the extra time department. I have tried to read new writers and have tried to encourage them, and I don't think that will cease until I am in the grave, or burned to ashes and distributed under a rose bush for dogs and insects to crap on.*

I have two responses to that.

Knowing Patrick's need to get things absolutely right—I'm sure that's the science teacher in him—I was less worried about Patrick's writing than Joe was about mine. In fact, I was curious. I'd read some of Patrick's work, but not a lot. But what I'd read until this point had been solid—even good.

Also, although I've had more than thirty books professionally published, I have yet to believe I'm done paying back. I'm sure no Joe Lansdale and will never be. I'm satisfied to be Weston Ochse, with all that entails. So, every year, I occasionally write an introduction for an author who I absolutely believe in and who I know will blow your mind. Because after all, now my words are tied inexorably to his, as is my reputation.

I've always found Patrick's personal life interesting, both in my social networking interactions and in person. Although he's not exactly Leon Battista Alberti, he seems to be on that glide path. Who is that, you ask? Alberti was a polymath or Renaissance Man. He was an Italian Renaissance humanist author, artist, architect, poet, priest, linguist, philosopher and cryptographer. It was also legend that he could jump over a man standing still. True, men were shorter in those days, but still that's #impressive.

Patrick is also impressive. Although he claims that he does everything because he is an 'ADD-riddled workaholic,' his output and contributions to the world, much of it unseen, could be described as Albertiesque. Patrick is an author, a beekeeper, a robotics coach, a teacher of physics, robotics, and American Sign Language, and also makes blistering hot saucy things with enough Scovilles to melt passing comets. He is not a one-trick pony, nor is he capable of being so. Patrick is a constantly moving target of intensity and output.

When asked about his writing inspirations, he said they range from Edgar Rice Burroughs to Niven / Pournelle / Barnes to NK Jemisin to Jonathan Mayberry to Dan Abnett and RA Salvatore and Kate Elliott. I find this an interesting literary swathe, but it explains how different the stories are in this collection. In fact, his stories are as diverse as they are interesting.

Perhaps the brightest of them all is the opening story, *In the Garden of Rusting Gods*. Not only is it critically well-written with his constantly musculating verbs, but what an incredibly inspired world he created. I can't help but believe that his descriptions were elevated by his personal knowledge of science. As sometimes happens, an author will create something so deep and multilayered that it could easily surpass being a story and become a full-fledged novel. I seriously hope that in the coming years I can return to the Garden of Rusting Gods and adventure for a much longer period of time. What he's done to our world is most terrible in invention, yet thought-provoking in how terrible it is.

Patrick also created an honest-to-God American detective story right out of Micky Spillane or Dashiell Hammett. Then there's a science fiction story that turns out to be a zombie story. Several intriguing ghost stories. And of course, there's a story about a beekeeper, but even that one has a precious twist.

Some of Patrick's writing stuck with me. In "A Creative Urge," he offers us sentences like this:

And yet, a knife of familiarity stabbed behind her eye at the twisted lines and unnerving curves that had once been her Tessie's limbs. A body couldn't lie like that, not in a Euclidean world, not in a universe where colors were merely spectral frequencies interpreted by primates who'd outgrown the jungle, where shapes defined a three-dimensional space of real things.

And this: *Between-creatures carried their shadows with them as they slinked from building to building, watched her approach with chittering anticipation.*

And even this:

And the moon, her moon, never moved, never once yielded its place in the sky. Yellow paint dripped from it to spatter across the gantries and bridges and towers of the silent city, Tess's broken light swallowed by the darkness that could not be satiated even as it dripped across Cassie's bridges and staircases, even as it dribbled into the dark, hungry seas that surrounded the impossible city. But still the moon dripped, and never did its paint-light wane.

The ability of Patrick to go from the graphic gore of a warzone to the beauty of this writing shows a writer flexing his muscles, ones that have been worked, and worked, until he is a literary athlete, perhaps like Leon Battista Alberti, ready to jump over a standing man, or at the very least entertain and inspire his readers.

I'm not going to spoil what is going to be a grand adventure.

In the end, these stories are for you, not for me. I've just been asked to introduce them and the author Patrick Freivald.

So, go forth, turn the page, or swipe to the left, however you are reading this.

I shall fade into the background, a mere Shakespearian moment, me in the spotlight as I introduce who you have come to see.

Fade to black.

Light is now on him.

Ready. Set. Go.

IN THE GARDEN OF
RUSTING GODS

IN THE GARDEN OF RUSTING GODS

Jaqueline eased her finger off the trigger as the god lumbered past the burned-out bus. Its hydraulic carapace whined with every shuddering step. The cable connecting it to the Worldstream snaked up to disappear into muddied air choked with the dying breaths of countless internal combustion engines. Massive metal claws lifted the rusted-out body of an ancient passenger car, and squeezed. It crumbled to pieces under its own weight to reveal nothing but shattered asphalt beneath. The behemoth lowed, long and sad, hungry.

Raising her eyes from the rifle scope, Jacq took in the devastated city, blackened shards of buildings clawing every horizon. Grit peppered her goggles, and memories of ash tickled her lungs through the ancient rebreather.

"It's going to hear the pumps." Ben's murmur, muffled by his gas , barely carried over the driving wind.

"Then it'll hear us." She patted the rifle. "Get ready."

"On my mark."

Kristen triggered the holofield, the last functioning technology that could camouflage their electromagnetic signatures from a god. When it worked. She vanished into a shimmering haze almost indistinguishable from the surrounding air.

The god slumped, a deliberate act for powered armor, a projection of grief that sparked the smallest hope in Jacq's heart that their years of reign might end, that someday children might garden in the sunlight above-ground, no longer hunted, free from the insatiable thirst of mechanical giants. She suppressed the glimmer with a deep breath and looked again through the scope.

Black polycarbonate hid the god's face, but thick nanofiber couldn't hide the extreme leanness of the creature housed within, or the shake in its spindly hands. Those palsied hands told Jacq all she needed to know; this god had foraged too long without feeding, and its desperation would make it predictable.

They'd buried the water pumps and set them to leak, the audio signature measured at negative ten decibels at ground level. Reclaimed water trickled out at regular intervals, quiet enough to hide from most gods at ten meters.

But this god straddled the garden. Too close, too risky.

Her finger slid onto the trigger, cold metal slick with machine oil.

"On my mark," Kris said. "Now!"

"Run," Jacq whispered.

Kris ran. The flicker of indistinct light caused the god to turn in her direction, sensors scanning for life.

"It's too close," Ben said. "You shouldn't—"

"Run, damn you."

"But Jacq—"

She fired.

Recoil turned her shoulder as the drillslug screamed from her rifle, the projectile's sixteen-thousand hertz whine drowning out the hum as the capacitors propelled it down quadrails at thirty gees. It hit the god's Higgs dampener with a blinding flash, microlegs flailing in a vain attempt to burrow into matter it hadn't reached.

The god reared in rage as the wriggling munition fell to the ground.

Ben ran.

The god advanced through the rubble, picking up speed with every step. It leapt a rotting pickup, arms spread to expose an array of empty microlaunchers. The ground shuddered as it landed.

Behind her, Ben screamed.

Don't look back.

A huge metal claw grazed the sniper's nest, and pebbles skittered down the slope to clatter against her helmet.

Ben faltered. Ten meters from the tube. Sixteen from the god.

He wasn't going to make it. Instead he stopped, fumbled for the death in his pocket. Too late.

Jacq closed her eyes and tried not to listen as his scream became a shriek. A pump chugged, and wet slurping overwhelmed Ben's agonized sobs. She didn't need to see the tangle of nanotubes writhing into his skin, didn't want to watch the light die from his eyes as the moisture and nutrients left his body. A sigh as the body hit the ground, light as a feather, not enough left to fertilize the garden.

Another sigh, contentment personified, blasted through the god's speakers.

It chuckled, sensors strangling data from the environment. Another step, almost a stumble, straight at Jacq. Adrenaline flooded her brain, bringing each slow, steady breath that much closer to a pant. Stopping, it sniffed the air, carbon dioxide sensors looking for telltale spikes that her rebreather hid, just as the scorched ground muffled her heat signature.

She held her breath. The slightest noise would kill her.

Her lungs burned. She struggled not to suck in precious oxygen. She wondered if her life, Ben's life, would buy the garden another day, buy her children another winter.

Gasping in a breath, Jacq rolled to her feet and ran. A high trill accompanied the movement, a drillslug impacting the Higgs dampener from off to the right. Two more followed it, and the distracted god's roar buffeted Jacq toward the escape tube.

The dull thud of a rocket launcher sounded from the left. A wall of air rocked her, then the noise hit, a furious blast. Then silence. She dove, and the tube swallowed her.

Jacq limped into the control room, helmet under her arm. Kate surveyed the monitors, the cables from her seven cranial jacks hanging in limp tangles. Jacq gave a curt nod in lieu of a salute.

"Where are we?"

Kate saluted, fist to her chest, eyes still fixed on the dozens of monitors displaying hijacked feeds and covert video cameras from the greater Rochester boneyard.

"We lost two, but saved the garden. Call it a win."

Jacq's breath caught in her throat. Ben owned his death—he should have run. Even so, guilt tore through her heart.

"Two?"

"Ben and Al. Good men."

Alfonso had fired the rocket. He'd saved her life. The god must have seen him before he made it to a tube. A gentle man, grandfatherly at home and clutch on a mission. Her children would cry for him. But Kris had survived.

"What about the god?"

"Seventy-three. Last records show him here nine years ago before moving west, before the Cleveland-Buffalo arcology went dark."

A colony of two thousand had lived in the ruins of the enormous building that covered what used to be Lake Erie. They'd ceased all radio contact and trade before Jacq had turned twenty. Everyone assumed they were dead.

Kate tapped the screen. "Frail then. Look at him now."

The god stumbled from one pile of detritus to another, rummaging through the remains of buildings before dropping to its knees, head bowed, serrated metal mouth open in a groan.

"This is before two catches. What about now?"

"This is live." Kate's smile turned vicious. "Seventy-three is dying."

A male voice replied, deep and sure. "So are we."

Jacq turned and put a fist to her chest. "Peter."

Peter returned the gesture. Almost sixty, but still strong and determined.

"You did good today, Jacq. The god spent so much time chasing us that he lost track of the garden. But it's not going to be enough. The blight has spread to garden nine, and it's only a matter of time before it hits the rest. We're out of fungicide. And time."

"UV kills it, right? Can we go deeper? Deep enough to disguise the heat from the bulbs?"

He put a hand on her shoulder. "You know we can't. Even if we had enough lights, which we don't, we don't have the power to light them. We need food, real food. A lot. We can't afford another cull."

On the monitor, Seventy-three remained on its knees. Jacq poured her hate into the grainy color image. The last cull had taken her children's father. Crippled by One-ninety-one and unable to work, James had said goodbye to their children, made tearful love to her one last time, and then went to the mulchers with his head held high.

She couldn't watch, couldn't listen, but had helped with the gardening all the same. Respect for the dead held no weight against the value of fertilizer.

With fewer mouths to feed, the four hundred survivors had lasted the winter. Before the blight hit they'd projected a good enough harvest to survive another without resorting to cannibalism. Now, with the gardens dying, maybe half would see the spring, if fed by the bodies of the dead.

"That beast." Jacq nodded at the screen. "He's slow, and getting slower. After feeding twice, he should be flush with energy, explosive."

Kate exchanged a look with Peter. "Of course. And?"

"And we're dead unless we find food, and there's none to find. Not here."

"Not anywhere."

Kate swept through the feeds, thousands of cameras and insect drones spanning hundreds of miles, from the poisoned shores of Lake Ontario to the hills of what used to be the Finger Lakes before arcologies had sucked them dry. Only five thousand people now lived in an area that had once housed eighty million.

"How many gods are left? A couple hundred?"

"Maybe," Kate said.

"There aren't enough hunters down here to satisfy that kind of appetite. We've—I've—got to go up there."

Peter grunted. "You can't be serious."

"I am." Jacq tapped the monitor with a fingernail, right above Seventy-three's enormous head. "If you can distract him, and I can take the holofield, I'll get to the Worldstream and see what I can bring back. It has to be … something."

Kate shook her head. "You can't climb that high. Nobody can."

"I'll need food, heavy clothes, and an oxygen tank. And a bonbon. I won't have to climb."

"The field isn't reliable. If they detect you—"

"Then I'm as dead as any airship that leaves the ground, and my children starve with the rest of you come winter. Which is what's going to happen anyway if I don't succeed."

Jacq locked eyes with Peter.

"I'm taking the holofield, and I'm going."

Peter nodded. "I'll get a volunteer."

They planted a new garden, six rows of twenty potatoes each, enough to make it believable. They let it grow a month, and then they sabotaged the pump. The gargle of water in the oil drew Seventy-three two days later, but instead of destroying the garden it squatted in the shadows, unmoving. At dawn it moved away, hunting, and returned the following night.

Kris smiled, and ran a hand across Jacq's close-cropped scalp.

"I guess it's time."

"There's another way." Jacq put a hand on her shoulder. "There has to be."

Someone had to look after her children. Their children, now.

They entwined fingers, Kris's dry, papery skin a familiar rasp against her own. And then Kris stood, fastening her tool belt.

"I'm sorry, love. But you need the distraction."

"I didn't mean for—"

Kris put a finger to Jacq's lips.

Jacq pulled away, tears flooding her eyes. "Then we call it off. Find another god."

Her face stung at the sudden slap.

"Don't." Kris held up her hand, ready to strike again. "If it weren't me, it would be someone else. You can't prioritize your own—"

Jacq wrapped her in a hug, squeezing too tight. She kissed her lips, tasted her on her tongue, and despaired. A lifetime of friendship and memories and love and hope cut to ribbons by her own foolish plan. The population had drawn straws, and Kris, her Kris, had come up short.

"Not you. Anyone but you."

Kris popped three pills into her mouth, dry-swallowing the bonbon. The capsules would dissolve in minutes, releasing the broad-based toxin that would destroy her over the course of agonizing hours. She extracted herself from the embrace and walked out.

"Go," Peter said. "You'll have no more than two minutes between consumption and self-destruct."

If this works.

Kris couldn't die in vain. She couldn't.

The world hazed to a dull smear of colors as Jacq triggered the holofield and followed Kris outside. It took two minutes to reach the pump. The god lurked in the shadow of a wrecked crane, its connection to the Worldstream hidden in haze.

Kris crept to the pump. Her hands, always steady, shook as she removed the bolts to the pump cover, and heaved the metal plate out of the way.

Always an actress, her Kris, to the final curtain call.

Seventy-three charged, speakers blaring a mindless, triumphant scream. Louder than life, louder than death. Kris jerked up, her glazed eyes crackled with red as the poison ruptured capillaries and liquefied organs.

A less desperate god would have seen the signs, would have shied away, let the poisoned meal rot on the ground.

A less desperate god would find another meal another day.

A thousand black tendrils snaked out of Seventy-three, finding Kris a split-second before the rest of its hulking body. Her flesh disintegrated as the god landed on top of her, every molecule of moisture leached from her in seconds.

The triumphant, primal roar became an inhuman, wailing scream.

Seventy-three stumbled to one knee, snorted, whipped around. The god screamed again, jerked sideways, flopped to its back. Its arms and legs shuddered as the toxin ravaged the creature within.

Jacq ran, the holofield smearing the world into a blur, and leapt. The snaking cable pulsed in her hands, a braided amalgam of wires and tubes that served as the god's link to the Worldstream, a network of gantries that enveloped the earth above the smog, held up by eldritch technologies she didn't understand. The cable quivered as she climbed, and she hoped the thrashing of the dying god would mask her own exertions, that her proximity to the tube would spare her the fate of everything else that had dared the sky.

The biomechanical toxin would spread through Seventy-three, cannibalizing the nanites in its blood and reproducing at an exponential rate. Fatal in hours to humans, it incapacitated a god in seconds. No one knew how long it took to kill them. On the few occasions a god fell for a bonbon, they'd self-destructed in minutes, their cable retracting through the smog.

Twin shockwaves buffeted Jacq as she pulled herself higher. She tangled her wrists through the cables before the concussive blow knocked her upward, away from the mushroom cloud that had reduced Seventy-three to ash and molten slag. Dangling, out of breath despite the oxygen tank, Jacq held on for life as the severed cable recoiled, carrying her into the sky.

The cable pulsed and shifted, contracting and rising ever upward. The gray-brown earth disappeared under a red-brown haze. A freezing wind tore at her clothes. She kept her breath steady, conserving oxygen, as the cable reeled her ever higher. A nervous knot in her gut blossomed over time from anxiety and grief to a great gnawing hunger, and still she rose.

Frost formed on her breath. The haze shrouding the world lightened to white-blue. An orange sphere blazed on the horizon, untouched by the corrupt miasma that smothered the world below. Ice glazed her goggles, blurring her view of the stars, pinpricks of light she'd only ever seen on video.

The Worldstream loomed above her, a giant, black lattice that encased the Earth ten thousand meters up, home to the gods. Enormous, spider-like constructs of plastic and metal scuttled on the underside. From each a tendril descended into the polluted atmosphere below, thousands of filaments connecting the Worldstream to the earth, just like the one on which she ascended.

Thousands of spider-things, not hundreds, each managing a cable that she presumed attached to a god. Four touched down in the ancient remains of Western New York, where over centuries the bedraggled survivors of mankind had managed to kill perhaps a dozen.

As she neared the top, she unclipped her harness from the cable, checked the holofield, and tensed. The spider-thing fed the cable into a dark hole, a continuous unweaving, a web in reverse. She leapt, hoisting herself through a gap in the lattice. The thing paid her no mind.

The holofield flickered, and through the light she took in the Worldstream.

Countless black spires clawed thousands of meters toward the stars, jagged needles under a dull white haze. Beneath them lay a junkyard, an endless expanse of defunct machinery where nothing grew, nothing moved. No insects fluttered in the thin air, no animals rummaged in the bitter cold. No Xanadu, no lush Eden from which the gods subjugated the worms beneath. Only death, despair, a garden of rust.

Even shielded from the shrieking wind, her body shuddered at the bone-jarring intensity of the cold.

She crept through the wreckage. The debris was human: hydraulic pistons and steel gears gummed to immobility, cracked rubber hoses bleached gray, scraps of broken chain link sagging between tarnished aluminum poles. Were it not for the honeycomb of massive holes leading to a fatal drop through the smog, it could be home.

Despite the oxygen tank, nausea stabbed her gut, something more than hunger. Her legs grew weak, her arms heavy, even as her toes and fingers ached with the biting, bitter cold. Perhaps the gods' realm was poison to mankind, a corruption so complete that nothing could live there.

For hours she shuffled through the endless boneyard, weakness leaching into every nerve, until at last a soft light drew her attention.

Taking shelter behind a giant crane, she peeked. A two-meter fence ringed an enormous, barren yard littered with shattered skeletons, white and brown bones frosted over from the extreme cold.

On the field of bones, men and women huddled near massive electric heaters, their only shelter a steel obelisk studded with small, pointed protrusions, streaked with rust. Their naked, sunburned bodies were mottled with crusted filth, their tight, frail skin exposing frail ribs. Cautious, uncertain, she waited, watching, trying to ignore her pulsing head.

A man approached a woman, pushed her down to all fours, and rutted with her. Both wore looks of bored disinterest. None of the others paid attention. None spoke.

A few minutes later, the same man approached the obelisk, put his mouth to a stud and suckled, grunting in rhythmic satisfaction. When he pulled back, a dribble of algal green spurted from the nipple, soaking his beard and splattering across his feet. He stepped away and sat near the blowers, staring out at nothing as they cast warm air overtop his lean body.

Food.

Jacq crept toward the fence. Ten feet from it, the sickly reek of body odor, shit and rot stopped her. Fumbling for the switch on her belt, she clicked it down. The holofield fizzled, and Jacq put her finger to her lips.

A woman saw her first, eyes wide.

Jacq nodded and spoke in a calm, controlled tone. "Hello."

The woman snarled, baring brown teeth. A man bellowed. The rest joined him, hooting in agitated, wordless excitement.

Jacq raised a hand. "Do you speak English? *Parlez-vous français?*"

A man marched forward, grabbed his crotch and shouted, tugging. Another shoved him out of the way and did the same. A brawl broke out. The first man laid into the second with his fists and feet, an artless, brutal beating that stopped when the second man fell into the fence.

A snap. Blinding light.

A mass of smoking meat littered the ground where the man had fallen, his body shattered and cooked by the electrical discharge. The fingers of his hand and severed wrist tangled in the fence, sizzling in a cloud of greasy smoke. The captives hooted and scrambled for the mess, shoving fistfuls of red into their mouths before retreating to the heaters.

Jacq backpedaled beneath the crane. Gorge rose in her throat and she choked back prickling, burning bile. Hands shaking, she re-activated the holofield.

She pulled a tracker from her pocket, ancient technology from before the gods.

She wrote a note, fifteen simple words, and signed it: "There is food here. I'll find how to get it. Give my children my love."

She rolled it, tucked it into the ring Kris had given her, and snapped the tracker to the steel band. It activated with a beep.

A short toss through the lattice and it disappeared into the smog.

The Worldstream shuddered beneath her feet.

A woman squealed in panic.

The captives scrambled to hide behind the obelisk, pushing and shoving to get in the back.

Another shudder, another cry.

A young man, no more than sixteen, stumbled from the crowd, helped forward by a shove.

A god came into view, cable trailing not upward but to a spider-thing behind it. Two more gods followed, their cables braided with the first.

She'd never seen more than one at a time, or witnessed a god with self-control. Yet these gods circled the pen as the captives cowered. At last the gods stopped. A black, snake-like tentacle rose from one's carapace.

The boy closed his eyes.

A thin trickle of piss leaked down his leg.

The filaments shot between the fence wires and into the boy, invading every cell, sucking out each molecule of water, every speck of nutrient. As the god fed, its cable pulsed into the spider-thing. The other two sighed, their contentment broadcast by speakers on their massive helmets.

They left the corpse, disintegrating skin over white bone already frosting over in the extreme cold, and trundled away. Jacq waited a minute, then lurched to her feet.

The world spun. She steadied herself, took a few deep breaths, and followed.

The gods passed another pen, then another, the same god feeding at each one. By the time the sun broke over the horizon, Jacq lost count of the number of corrals, but the legions of starving human cattle dwarfed the population surviving on the earth's surface.

Near midday, the gods approached an enormous hall of ribbed beams leading into the base of a spire.

Their chests split open, and Jacq suppressed a gasp. Folding outward, the carapaces revealed humanoid shapes, small and wiry and black. Shaking hands reached up to pull away metal carapaces.

Form-fitting helmets peeled off to reveal shriveled, liver-spotted faces under matted white hair. First, a woman—not a god at all, but human—spoke, her dialect similar to that spoken on ancient vids.

"Not sure what the commotion was about, but a good feeding, anyway."

The two men, both as bald and liver-spotted as she, nodded. One clapped her shoulder with a hydraulic whine, a mechanical imitation of Kris and Jacq after a successful mission.

"Skinnier every month, but still invigorating. I could go for a few more to be honest, dear."

She had eaten, but the man had found the meal delicious. A dark hope wriggled into Jacq's heart.

The other man replied.

"Couldn't we just have a few more?"

The woman shook her head. "No."

"But mom—" His whine set Jacq's teeth on edge.

"You're seven hundred years old! Stop acting like a child. The hunters are failing their quotas by ninety percent, and get just enough to survive. This isn't last century—we're subsidizing them, not the other way around, and it's ridiculous. A million cattle can't keep us all fat, not indefinitely. And they're skinnier every month. Do the math, and quit your whining."

His shoulders slumped. "Yes, mother."

They walked deeper into the spire, fading into the distance. As the holofield flickered again, Jacq decided against following. Instead she backed out, found shade between the hulking wrecks of two tracked vehicles, and let exhaustion take her.

It took her a day to find another spider-thing, and hours of waiting before she could examine a cable up close. As the god hunted on the surface, the spider kept the cable from tangling, moving it on sliding tracks under the Worldstream floor to accommodate the god's roaming. Those tracks fed into a larger cable, which fed an even larger one. The network snaked back into the city of spires, hundreds of pulsing lines transporting … what?

She peeled the cladding from one, stripping away insulation with a knife to find copper wire. Others held flexible glass, fiber optics pulsing data at the speed of light. The thickest bled when she cut it, a spurt of hot red fluid that smelled of iron and meat. She pulled out her breather, and tasted the liquid.

Blood. Fat. Marrow.

Her mouth watered even as her stomach roiled. She covered the hole with her thumb, cutting off the spurting stream.

A laugh ruptured the silence: her own. She understood at last why the gods self-destructed when they fell victim to the bonbon. A single biomechanical network, a globe-spanning circulatory system sucking the life from the planet, couldn't stomach such a nanomechanical threat.

The ancient vids spoke of invasion, but they never said by whom, or by what. All her life she'd assumed—everyone had assumed—the gods were alien, or extradimensional. Yet she'd climbed to the heavens to find them all too human.

Greed. Lust. Gluttony.

A few elevating themselves over billions in desperate squalor, consuming them so they might live for centuries.

Enough.

She drank, forcing down the nutrients, suckling at the cable until it stitched itself back together, cut it and drank again. Sated, belly full for the first time in years, she set out toward a mission even more important than food.

The cables grew fatter and fatter. She walked for days, toward the tallest of the distant spires. At some point she'd run out of food, then water, the ever-thicker cables resisting her ability to cut them, even with her best knife. Every step took all her effort, though over time her piercing headache faded, replaced by the aching cold. Frigid wind cut through her clothes, and she'd long since lost feeling in her toes. The merciless sun burned exposed skin to blisters, and frost numbed it to an aching nothing. She mumbled through cracked lips; to her absent children and their dead father. To Kris, who had loved her when everything else had withered, whose sacrifice had killed Seventy-three. Her words half-formed in a mouth too dry to speak, and died on the wind.

The holofield had failed on the third day. She'd let it fall, another piece of garbage on a world buried by it. Her oxygen gave out, and she let that fall, too. The thin air left her light-headed, delirious, counting every step from zero.

The largest spire stretched into space, black on black, an arrogant defiance of gravity and sense. The cables joined at its base, tens of thousands of them, a snaking mass connected to a bulbous tank the size of a city block. Huge pumps shuddered all around it, transporting precious fluid from and to withered gods all over the planet.

Jacq searched for a way in. A single steel door stood in the shadows, emblazoned with a peeling painting of a flag. Eighty white stars on blue, with thirteen red and white stripes, it looked regal, proud, significant. Something to adorn the uniforms of heroes. As she turned the wheel on the bulkhead, a klaxon wailed. She ignored the alarm and let the darkness inside swallow her.

A network of gantries crisscrossed above huge vats, each connected to the next by rust-stained pipes. A single flight of metal stairs, too small for a god, exhausted her, but she made it to the top before falling to her knees. Panting, light-headed, she looked down into an open tank, a red maw of steaming blood and precious fluids.

She slid shaking fingers into her pocket, pulled out a small bottle.

More than Ben had managed before Seventy-three had taken him.

Three pills. White, unassuming.

So tiny a thing to make a world without gods.

Metal shrieked across metal. Sunlight streaked inside as a dozen gods tore the room apart. The world shook as they blasted through railings and walkways toward her.

She pressed on the cap, turned it. The plastic lid clattered through the grate.

A thousand black tendrils pierced her body, lifted her from the ground, arms spread wide over the vat.

As the light faded, her hand went limp. Gods screamed as the bottle fell into the crimson pool below.

She thought of her starving children, and smiled.

FORWARD BASE FOURTEEN

A warning blip chimed, and a green dot turned red in Sarah DeSouza's vision.

Droplets streaked her visor, fogged opaque in the New Phoenix humidity so that only her HUD gave any useful information—temperature, vitals, team position, the seventeen rounds left in her magazine, and an endless stream of data from the trackdrones stationed around Forward Base Fourteen. Sweat matted her hair under the helmet, the pungent tang of wet dog and body odor an unwelcome reminder that their last supply drop came too long ago, and with too little.

"DeSouza, status?" Sergeant Brett Jackson's voice in her ear carried a razor's edge buried under gravel, both harder and more fragile than months past.

"Track nine went offline." She punched directions into the keyboard and fine-tuned them through the neural link. "I'm shifting eight and ten to cover the sweep."

"Battery?"

"Likely. It's been leaking H-gel since the last attack." Their most vital and scarcest resource, hydrogen stabilized in a fire-retardant gel ran the microfusion reactors that powered everything from their rail guns to the trackdrones to the AC units and refrigerators, to the massive terraformers looming in skies a thousand miles to the south.

Not that they had any AC or refrigerators, or more than a dozen trackdrones left.

She licked her lips. "When do you think they'll hit us, Sergeant?"

"Server's offline, private. Predictive models—"

"When do *you* think, Sergeant?"

Jackson sighed. "Any time. They're wearing us down before the headshot." He paused. "And we're about as worn down as we can get."

Her heart skipped. "You think we have a chance?"

He said nothing for far too long. "No. Do your duty, private. It's all that's left."

Jackson and DeSouza, the last of twenty-eight personnel sent to relieve FB14, had survived the past few weeks by blind luck. The Takers had broken their line too many times, carried off too many bodies, or worse, infected them with biomechanical parasites and left them behind. Bodies that came back, armed and augmented with biomechanical appendages a generation ahead of United States technology.

A technician, DeSouza managed the sixty-eight trackdrones slaved to her neural link, so she did more good inside HQ than out in the thick of the fighting.

Eleven. Not sixty-eight. Eight months prior they'd had sixty-eight well-armed and spit-polished trackdrones, and another two dozen wingers patrolling the sky. Seven months of boredom, patrols through the endless forests, defending the supply routes from an enemy that never came.

Then the sky lit up over the horizon, too far to see the mushroom cloud, too far to hear the roar, or smell the burning concrete and bodies. That light severed contact from New Houston and from orbital command. Two weeks later the satlink went down for good, and the attacks had started.

"Private?" Jackson's voice startled her out of the reverie.

"Yes, sergeant?"

"You can gather wool when you're dead. Stay alert."

"Yes, sergeant."

Static scrabbled across the network, and scattered through it fragments of words.

Eyes wide, Sarah cranked the volume and patched it through the PA system. "Sergeant, you getting this?"

Voices. Human voices, the first they'd heard in weeks and in snippets too short to make out. A sob escaped her throat, unbidden and unwanted, and she choked down those that followed.

"I read. Triangulate?"

Her chuckle held no mirth. "I'm not signals. You know how?"

He appeared in the doorway, tear-streaked cheeks glistening, a pistol forgotten in one hand, a crumpled photograph in the other. He rushed the console, dropping the weapon on a chair on the way by, and fiddled with knobs, dark muscles bulging under his tight white T-shirt.

The rich, burnt-wood smell of bourbon filled the room, with oniony human odor beneath. *Thanks for sharing, jerk.* She frowned at the uncharitable thought, and the smell.

Behind Sergeant Jackson's back, Sarah picked up his weapon. One round chambered, nothing in the magazine, the grip clammy with sweat from being held too long. She plucked the picture from the console and smoothed it out. A chocolate-skinned woman cradled a black-haired baby to her breast while Jackson beamed with a father's pride.

A woman's voice filled the room. "Forward Base Twelve, do you copy?"

Jackson leaned in and pressed the COM button. "This is Forward Base Fourteen. We are low on supplies and expecting attack. Do you read me?"

"Forward Base Twelve, this is Eagle Command, do you copy?" she repeated.

Leaning in, he raised his voice. "Eagle Command, this is Forward Base *Fourteen* requesting immediate evac."

"Forward Base Twelve, this is Eagle Co—" Her voice exploded in a burst of static.

"Fuck!" Jackson slammed his fist on the table. "Eagle command, do you copy?"

He tried for hours, in turn broadcasting a distress signal and sweeping for replies. None came. Night fell, and with it the track-drones switched to thermal imaging in her mind.

A ragged moan erupted from Jackson's throat, followed by rasping hyperventilation.

Sarah stood and backed away, tucking the pistol into the back of her pants. "Tomorrow, Sergeant. They'll find us tomorrow. We're going to be okay."

He lifted his face from his hands and stared at her with blood-shot eyes devoid of hope. "Give me my weapon."

She shook her head. "I think it's best I hold onto it for tonight."

"Private, give me my weapon."

"No, sergeant. You can court martial me when we—"

The chair flipped as he came out of it in a bull's charge. She spun, but not fast enough.

Air blasted from her lungs as he checked her into the wall. Strong hands crushed around her throat. She clawed at his wrists, gaping and gasping and pleading with unseen eyes. Face twisted in hatred and despair, he screamed at her, hot spittle spraying her face, burnt wood and ethanol and unbrushed teeth. "Give me my gun!"

Her knee glanced off his thigh.

Pain shredded her thoughts as he slammed his forehead down on the bridge of her nose. Eyes rolling back, she balled one hand into a fist. She punched, but with no leverage it bounced off of his muscled abdomen. He screamed, slamming her head into the wall with each word.

"Give. Me. My. Gun. You. Fucking. Cunt."

The world hazed to a muddy red as she groped back. Hot agony shrieked up her arm as her fingers crushed between the pistol and the wall. It slipped free and she brought it around. Rail weapons make no sound as they fire, save for the click of the trigger.

The recoil ripped the gun from her hand, and in the deafening silence Brett fell back. She gasped precious air into her lungs and dropped to her hands and knees. Her pointer and middle fingers bent at unnatural angles, but she couldn't feel them through the consuming fire in her chest.

Slumping to the side, she rolled her eyes up to her assailant.

Brett lay back on her cot, only his legs visible over the side, but hot gore steamed on the wall behind him.

Gagging, she rolled back up to her hands and knees, then stayed there, light-headed, to regain her equilibrium. Thick tendrils of bloody snot streamed from her mouth and nose. She coughed, spat, coughed again.

And as the world slowed its spinning, she stood, and looked down at Sergeant Jackson.

The bullet had entered under his sternum and traveled upward, tearing a gaping hole that left pieces of ribs and shoulder behind him on the bed. A pungent mix of blood and fresh shit filled the room. Her gorge rose, then chunky red-and-brown vomit erupted from her mouth to join the sticky mess.

Bile burning her throat, she grabbed the cot one-handed and dragged it into the hall. That done, she sat back down at her desk to monitor the drones.

Drone two died at three a.m., and drone seven an hour later. They hadn't been damaged.

She fanned the rest out to cover her escape route and grabbed what she could before the Takers breached the perimeter.

Boots crunched across generations of leaves that choked out any undergrowth. Sarah carried everything she could manage toward the rising sun and Forward Base Twelve: two bladder canteens—one of clean water, the other the remnants of the bourbon taken from the small shrine in his room where Jackson had planned to kill himself—a drone power core and six feet of heavy wire, one microfusion antipersonnel mine, and a pistol with four rounds. The rifle had more ammo, but she couldn't manage it as well with broken fingers. Firing a pistol left-handed might work. Might.

The world rocked as Forward Base Fourteen's power core detonated. A scaled-up version of the drone cores, her training at scuttling the small equipment translated exactly to the larger machine. She stumbled on, one foot in front of the next, her HUD displaying GPS information and highlighting obstacles in her path.

Three days to Forward Base Twelve, and possible rescue.

One foot in front of the next. One foot in front of the next.

Her HUD blinked red, once: enemy signature detected. Ducking behind a tree, she scanned left and right. A double triangle, red on red, highlighted a dark shape under a fallen log. She staggered toward a babbling stream, not having to feign her exhaustion or thirst.

Kneeling, she put the pistol on the ground and winced as she lowered to take a drink, eyes closed to track the stealthy shuffling behind her. Her right hand throbbed in time with her racing heart, and the cool water held a metallic hint of blood.

The rustle turned into a charge. She rolled left and choked up the pistol, firing twice at the humanoid shape flying toward her. The double-tap took it center-of-mass at point-blank range. Puffs of black-red hydraulic fluid sprayed the trees behind the Taker, and it shrieked with a voice not its own.

Corporal Nedel's body collapsed and writhed as the Taker's biomechanical dendrites and hydraulic muscle writhed and squirmed to repair the damage to its host. She rolled to her feet, stepped forward, and put her foot on its back to force it still.

As she shot the neural cortex embedded into his lower spine, a tendril stabbed from between its ribs, an icy lance that punctured straight through her boot and the foot inside. Grunting at the sudden pain, she reached down and pulled out the ropy black mass. It came free with a slippery, wet feeling, but no blood leaked from the wound.

She looked around, using the HUD to highlight any further danger. The woods stood quiet under a blue sky, a beauty she hadn't noticed in her determined run toward Forward Base Twelve. She sat next to the body and pulled off her boot and sock.

And gasped.

Tiny black filaments writhed around the wound.

"Oh, fuck you," she snarled. She looked up at the sky and laughed, a mirthless despair given voice. Her eyes fell to the pistol. A single round remained. She sighed and murmured, "You can't have me you sons of bitches, but I'm not going out like that either."

A quick search of Nedel's body told her what she didn't want to know: he carried no food, no painkillers, and no knife.

It took more effort than she'd imagined to remove a belt with two broken fingers, and more to loop it and twist a long stick through it. Working methodically, she hummed a lullaby her mother used to sing, something to distract her from the gruesome task at hand.

She worked a single strand of copper wire into a loop, one end twisted around an oblong rock, a cave man electrician's garrote. She took off her pants, tightened the belt tourniquet above her knee and the makeshift cutter below it, then clenched a stout stick between her teeth, and took a deep breath.

She rolled her weight onto the stick to hold it in place, grabbed the rock, and lay back so she wouldn't have to look. Eyes squeezed shut, she bit down on the stick and mumbled around it.

"I'm not becoming one of you motherfuckers. I'm not."

She twisted and slid the rock back and forth. Her skin parted in a line of hot fire. Another twist, another slide, another jolt of crippling madness and pain. And another, and another. Blinded by tears, she tried not to hyperventilate, but passed out multiple times. She'd wake, crying, and grab the rock. And twist, and slide. Twist, and slide. Even as the circle tightened through the tendons and ligaments of her knee. She couldn't give up; she had work to do. Twist, and slide.

An eternity later the leg came off, a relief that brought no relief. She sighed and forced her cramped fingers to open, dropping the makeshift saw. She drank the whiskey, three whole swallows of soothing heat, and didn't bother to pour any on her wound. No point in disinfecting a dead woman.

She pulled the antipersonnel mine to her and removed the cover. Wires snaked from the fusion core to a customizable trigger mechanism next to a sticker that boasted a kill radius of sixty meters. Left-handed, she discarded the button and tripwire, and instead attached the pressure switch. The sun crested and crept toward the horizon. "Come and get it, you bastards."

Fever burned through her. She struggled to think, to move, to remember her last act of patriotism and bravery: take as many of those bastards as she could on her way out.

As twilight darkened the woods, it took all her effort to roll sideways, slide the mine and pressure switch under her back, and roll on top of them. The switch primed with a dull snap.

Nothing to do now but live. Takers would ignore a corpse, but injured humans drew them like flies to honey.

Her eyes closed despite her protests.

She woke to flashes of light. Biomechanical shrieks in the distance answered dull clicks above her, Takers using human throats to voice their pain and outrage. One eye flickered open, the most she could manage.

Two men in forest camo and helmets stood over her, rail rifles barking silent death into the surrounding woods with casual, brutal efficiency.

"Confirmed alive and uninfected," one said. "Send medevac ASAP."

"We're moving out. Fall back on my position," the other said.

A chorus of acknowledgments slithered through her neural link.

"No, you can't," she said. But nothing came out of her dry mouth. She tried to force her tongue through cracked lips, but the thick, desiccated muscle wouldn't respond. A knot in her lower back pulsed with the gunfire, a shrieking reminder of the death waiting beneath her.

The first man knelt, fired two shots, and looked down at her. Her own face, wan and wasted, stared back out of his mirrored visor. "Ma'am, you're going to be okay." She tried to swat his hand away as he pressed a narcopatch to her neck.

The world swam, soft and warm. Her eyes fluttered as more men backed to stand over her, weapons chattering, a full squad of soldiers in tactical response gear.

"Back!" she tried, but only a giggle came out, a narcotic-fueled manic amusement.

If they heard, they didn't react. A Brightsky-pattern transport swooped low above them, chrome steel wings blanketing the sky thirty feet above the treetops, propellers blasting them with a downward wash of air. Two squads of men hung from their deployment pods, weapons flashing as they fired through the canopy.

She slapped at the soldiers as they knelt and reached for her.

"You can't . . . ."

"It's okay, ma'am. You're safe now. We've got them on the run all across the sector. You're a hero."

She shook her head. "No!" It came out clear and strong.

"Yeah. You are."

The medic smiled and lifted her.

THE STAR

"You suck!" rang out over the feedback and the drums, followed by a chorus of boos and jeers. Dominic flinched as lukewarm beer spattered his pants, the plastic cup tumbling away to fall behind the amplifier. His band finished the song under a growing din of hateful discontent, and he stared at his own feet and spoke into the microphone.

"Thank you! We're , and—"

"And you suck balls!" The massive biker-looking dude in the front row leaned on a sun-leathered barfly, his gray-black beard wet with cheap beer and spittle. She flipped off the band and grabbed her crotch. He followed suit, rough hand sliding over hers to give a comical goose. The crowd laughed.

"Damn," Phil muttered, pretending to tune his guitar.

Jason hammered the bass drum, the unrelenting beat an introduction to a song they'd just added to their lineup, one of four original tunes in the set. The bass walked, almost bluesy, a contrast to the punk-metal tempo and the Pink Floyd-style rhythm guitar riff, exactly as they'd practiced until Phil botched his intro and came in a measure too late. Dominic sang the first notes, stopped, tried to pick it up on the second line, but Phil didn't adjust. The melody withered in his throat.

The lights died, and with them the speakers, and the owner stepped up shaking his head, hands raised. "Sorry, boys, but if I let you keep playing we're not even going to make overhead. Pack up and get out."

Ken faltered on the bass, his glassy eyes scrunching confusion. An awkward grin spread across his face. "Did the power go out?"

The crowd cheered as Ian Grant's hit single, "Big Green," blared through tinny speakers over the bar, drumming out the pop beat and the hometown hero's singing, still as smooth and intense as the day Dominic had met him, hooting out love songs—in harmony—to the girls on the sidewalk. They'd endured the rolled eyes and giggles with the pathological lack of shame only possessed by seventh-grade boys. Carefree days crushed under the weight of celebrity and envy.

Looking down to hide the wetness in his eyes, Dominic kicked their blurry set list across the floor then stalked off stage. The insult-to-injury stabbed at his throat, and a gagging reflex just kept down the soggy chicken wings and limp fries he'd gotten from the bar after sound-check. Stomach roiling, he lurched for the door.

Dom had been the songwriter, Ian the singer. Gravel on silk, nothing could match the raw, jagged hurt Ian's voice had developed their senior year. Rolling in girls and money his whole life, nothing about it came from personal truth. But on the stage and in the studio no one could hear the lie. Nothing said "show biz" like false truths.

Rock stars.

They'd dreamed it together, chased it together, shared late nights and long days and girls and drugs and boys and sometimes each other and when the studios came for their demo tape they took the singer and left the songwriter behind to rot in the rocky ground of Bend Creek, Indiana. Gravel on silk, the sound of heaven, the sound of hell. Dominic got in the van, slammed the door, and screamed into his hands.

"Did you see this shit?" Phil shoved the flyer into his face, the eighty millionth Dominic had seen since that morning. Ian Grant, July 9, Bend Creek Pavilion. The international superstar would grace his hometown with a performance before leaving on the European leg of his world tour to promote "Small Town Cannibal." Dominic's idea, brooding, blood-soaked metal twisted and reborn through the sanitized, homogenous imaginings of corporate suits into flavorless electronic pop.

"I saw it." Dominic dropped his fork into the congealed glop that passed for a sausage omelet at two on a Wednesday afternoon and didn't bother raising his eyes. "So what?"

"Maybe he'd let us open for—"

"I am NOT opening for Ian Grant."

Jason squeezed into the booth next to him, scooping up a handful of soggy, cheesy eggs and shoveling it into his mouth. "I thought," he sucked on his calloused fingers, "you wanted to be famous."

Dominic lifted his eyes to Phil's, half-obscured by stringy, dirty-blond hair the guitarist thought made him look like Curt Cobain. "This an ambush?"

Even overruled at three-to-one, he'd never do anything with Ian Grant, not even a photo-op, not ever. To hell with band rules.

"Nah, man, Ken ain't here so there's no vote." Phil sat, waving off the waitress as she approached, sunken eyes hopeful for a tip she'd probably blow on a bump of crystal. "We knew you wouldn't go for it. Just thought maybe you'd hook us up, get us backstage."

"Why would I get us backstage?"

Jason stole a lump of sausage from a puddle of grease. "So we can introduce ourselves, maybe meet his manager."

"I don't want—"

"We're not talking about you. We're talking about us."

Seething betrayal ravaged his nerves. Of course Deathsmack sucked; half the members would sell out their integrity for a taste of money or fame. They had no passion for the music, for the craft. "You want what he has."

"So do you. Asshole." Phil got up and stalked out of the booth. Jason joined him. "So do you."

The door jangled shut.

The shrieking of delirious fangirls jabbed ice picks behind his eyes, almost painful enough to distract him from the stink of perfume and sweat, the tang of marijuana and the cloying Victoria's Secret body spray used to mask it. And the concert wouldn't start for another two hours, Ian Grant an hour after that.

Dominic cut through the line to the side door and rapped a "shave and a haircut" with his knuckles. A black man the size of a house peered out, took in their back-stage passes, and stepped aside just enough to let them through.

"Hey, we're Deathsm—"

"Down the hall." The bouncer closed the door and leaned against it. "He's expecting you."

Ken twirled past framed posters depicting concerts from decades past, legends and icons lost to drugs or age or an inability to sustain their creativity against the ravages of time. The rest followed, Jason and Phil playing it outwardly cool. Dominic just managed not to throw up as Ian Grant appeared in a doorway, teeth too white, brown hair too perfect.

The superstar shook hands, spending just enough time with each man before moving to the next, leaving them with a taste and wanting more. The world grew dark as he enveloped Dominic in a hug, crushing his heart and bones to lifeless jelly before pulling back and looking at him with eyes that shone with inner light.

"Dom. It's good to see you, man. It's been too long."

Dominic choked down years of abandonment, jealousy, and impotent regret. "Yeah. Too long."

The "green room" consisted of two leather couches and a coffee table piled with local barbeque, chicken and pork stacked high next to thick, crusty bread, and not a vegetable in sight. At Ian's insistence the band tucked in, everyone but Dominic chewing between excited questions about the road, the studios, and the groupies. His stomach lurched, hot bile tickling the back of his throat.

"It's not like you think." Ian's grin fell from his face. "It's exciting, but it's pretty lonely, and it's easy to spend too much on fans and fun. You got to work to save anything, 'cause this won't last forever."

Jason waggled his eyebrows. "But the groupies?"

"Are part of the problem." His eyes bored into Dominic's. "Nobody just wants to be your friend. Everybody you meet wants something, an angle, an introduction, a collaboration, maybe just a star-fuck. Even people from back home."

"Fuck, man, Dom didn't even want to do this. We—"

"I'm sure he didn't. Enjoy the food, and the show." Ian stood, brushed nonexistent lint from his jeans, and walked out.

Phil snorted. "You really hate each other, don't you?"

"Yes," Dominic said. *And no and never.*

Phil, Jason, and Ken left to enjoy the show. Dominic moseyed down the back hall, where a security guard's eyes wandered to his backstage pass before returning to stare straight ahead. A light flickered from a dark room to his left.

Eyes rose to meet his, black surrounded by whites turned blue by the screen of her phone. Soft, high cheekbones accentuated black lips and straight, dark hair, the only parts of her not lost to shadow.

"You must be Dominic." Harsh consonants pulled him into the room, an ancient accent from another continent yet somehow English. Her screen went black, plunging the room into a nothing that swallowed light from the door.

"How do you know that?" The darkness around her devoured his voice, muffled it to a whimper.

"I smelled you on him when we first met. I never forget a smell." Her tone shifted, became conversational. "Come in, have a seat."

The words dragged his feet and he approached, sank onto the lukewarm leather. Scant light emanating from the doorway betrayed nothing of her form, though her warmth crawled against his shoulder and thigh, her scent a mélange of mint and jasmine.

He cleared his throat. "So who are you, again?"

Hot breath tickled his neck. "He calls me Polyhymnia. I'm his sacred voice, and in this age what is more sacred than sex and money? I'm everything you wanted but he stole. From his mother, from Mr. Charles, even from you, taken for his own as he abandoned you to this … life."

Confused, Dominic pulled away, but on the soft cushion her leg fell against his.

Mr. Charles had left a love note for his wife and swallowed a month's worth of oxycodone the summer before their senior year. The school hadn't replaced the beloved music teacher, instead assigning Mrs. Logan to the junior and senior high chorus as well as the bands. The whole program had suffered. Still suffered.

"What do you mean?"

Her low giggle shivered down his spine, stroked his groin, entered and infused him, a shudder of pleasure made sound. "Come on, Dom. You've felt the loss since he gained his voice, and your talent withered. You can't believe it's a coincidence."

"How … could it not be?"

Her voice grew hard. "I am not coincidence."

Melodies flooded him, harmonies and counter-harmonies, dark chords and bright trills, raw, screaming emotion on modern instruments. He gasped as they engorged him, cried out as they faded. "No, wait! I need—"

Her lips met his, breasts pressed against him, and her breath filled his lungs, sweet cherries and rich, dark chocolate, and a hint of something acrid.

She pulled away, panting, and whispered. "Take me away. I am not his, I don't belong to this. Free me, and I'll give you everything."

"What are you talking about?"

A tornado of images shone in her wide pupils; screaming fans and hotel rooms, Deathsmack merchandise on Walmart shelves and in teenagers' rooms, red carpets and fast cars and Hollywood mansions, and at the center Dominic screaming into the microphone.

He pulled back, gasping. Then he lifted her from the couch, light as a feather, heavier than the cloud of depression that had become his reality, and ran.

Polyhymnia—Nia—whispered to him, and in the wake of her voice his imagination exploded across the page. Darkness and hunger made sound in his mind, flowing through his hands to ink dots on stanzas, chords and lyrics shining forth in a brilliance he'd never known he'd possessed. Stacks of pages had piled up, and at some point the phone had stopped ringing—he could only assume his boss had given up, figuring out that he'd quit.

Blinding light blasted across his vision. He squeezed his eyes shut, cracked them, and turned toward the door.

Ken stood, hand still on the light switch, eyes wide. "Dude. You need a shower."

Grinning, he leapt to his feet, stepping over piles of laundry and scattered music sheets to grab his friend by the shoulders.

"And to brush your teeth."

Dominic nodded, eyes wide and bloodshot in the reflection of Ken's glasses. "Yeah, sure. But we need to make a demo. Like, now."

Ken pulled back. "Shower, teeth, maybe a little food. Then we'll talk about a demo."

Dominic's stomach gnawed at his spine, and he swooned against the door. How many days had Nia whispered to him, driven him with her furious passion? He had no idea, and he didn't care.

"Okay, yeah."

After the last chord faded the sound tech killed the microphones. "That. Guys. That was incredible. I don't think I've heard anything that good in … in ever."

They high-fived, hugged, celebrated with beer and chicken wings at the local tavern.

Jason raised his glass in a toast, eyes on Dominic. "This is you, man. You're a freaking genius."

Glasses clinked. Dom ignored the sour taste that accompanied the smooth draft pouring down his throat. He slammed down the glass, got up, and stumbled to the bathroom, a mess of graffiti and filth under a single flickering light bulb.

She met him in the stall, pulling back his hair as he threw up, semi-liquid chunks splattering the unflushed mound of paper and shit in the stainless steel bowl. His stomach settled but his mind roiled.

"Are you in my head?"

"No, but if you let me in you would see that what I've given is but a pale shadow of what we could be."

He raised his hands, palms up, to the glamor of their surroundings. "I could stand a little less of this glory."

Her sigh breathed solace through the stink of vomit and piss. "We've only just begun."

Dominic threw his sweat-soaked black T-shirt into the crowd with a triumphant scream, bowing as they roared their approval. The moment the lights died he stalked off the stage. Their energy filled him to bursting. Dark filaments flickered in and out of substantiality, grasping, dragging him toward *her*. With a pirouette he tromped down the hall into the back parking lot, fumbled open his trailer door, then collapsed face-down on the couch inside. Throat raw, lungs burning, heart thundering, he couldn't keep the grin from his lips.

"He died tonight." Nia's voice squirmed through the dark, crawling across his veins and into his blood, sucking at the adulation, basking in the worship of the crowd.

"I know. I felt it during 'Midnight's March.'" Second song of the third set, a discordant wall of sound with symphonic accompaniment. It roared with new life at the moment of Grant's death.

Ian's career had ended as meteorically as it started. A competent musician, he'd never had the raw talent necessary for stardom, and when Dominic had stolen away with Polyhymnia mid-tour, his popularity plummeted and his fans had abandoned him, followed by his sponsors and then his label. In three months he'd snorted, injected, and drank his fortune to nothing, then spent two years in and out of rehab and jail.

"How?"

"Robbing a grocery with an Airsoft gun. The clerk had a shotgun. It will be on the news in due time."

He said nothing, content to give his former friend a moment of silence, and for once in thirty months Nia didn't take the last word.

In the hall a raucous crowd bumbled past the dressing room, his band and their entourages and a new stream of hot young groupies, the best on offer in … wherever they were. They'd be on buses the next morning and hit another city, then another. Phil, Jason, and Ken would enjoy the night, drinking and laughing and fucking, and he'd write their next hit, and their next, burning through Polyhymnia's limitless passion in an orgy of creativity.

Her passion. Her creativity.

Stolen by Ian Grant through black magic Dominic didn't understand, then regifted when Nia had abandoned his old friend.

She'd never given him an indication that she'd do the same to him, claimed Dominic had rescued her and that she'd serve him as long as he needed her. But her power rankled, her gifts offended his sense of pride. He had everything he'd ever wanted—fame, fortune, respect, a life doing what he loved—but "fraud" and "charlatan" skirted the dark corners of his heart, black rats gnawing at his happiness, denying him contentment with every greedy nibble.

He'd had talent before Ian had stolen it from him, some talent, enough to get by, maybe enough to climb the charts. But nothing like this. He'd written—she'd written—a thousand songs with his hand, stashed away in drawers and on remote servers, backed up and protected from fire or malice. A lifetime of work penned in two years of insomnia, all of it brilliant beyond measure, enough to create as many albums as he'd ever want. If only—

Nia sighed, a tickle on the back of his neck, a lingering promise across his skin. "He thought he didn't need me, too, in the end. Thought he could sustain what he'd taken from me, tricked himself into believing the lies of the mob. That he mattered, that he was worthy."

The TV flickered to life, muted, bathing the black-curtained trailer in a harsh LED glow. A talking head spoke in front of an ambulance. In the corner of the screen, Grant's latest mug shot scowled, skin sallow, cheeks gaunt, haunted eyes sunken and desperate. The splash banner scrawled SINGER IAN GRANT DEAD AT 24 across the bottom of the screen.

Her confident whisper nipped at his ear. Her fingertips stroked his naked back. "What more evidence do you need? He stole what I've given you freely, and though that makes you righteous where he was not, it doesn't make you worthy. So be with me, use me, let me inside you, and enjoy the life I've given. Don't throw it away on an arrogant whimsy."

"It's not *whimsy* to be my own man." He spat the word out so as not to choke on the dismissive, condescending syllables. "I …"

He swallowed. Memories swirled with her voice in his ears, a haze of passion more glorious than sex, more sensual than the wildest of Deathsmack's already-legendary backstage parties. He couldn't remember a time before her smell, a breath before her taste on his lips, a night without her as his moon—his star.

"Don't say it." Her whisper turned almost petulant as she repeated the same old request. "You could be so much more than you are, not less. A sun blazing across the Earth, scorching all who come too near your brilliance. Don't push me away. Don't discard me. Don't leave me in your wake. Take me into you. Let me *be* you, and ride with me into unimaginable glory."

And that was it. He'd lost himself in her, giving everything he could without losing himself completely, and she only wanted more.

"I need to do this. Without you."

"You don't."

"I need to do it myself."

"You can't."

"I am. And I need you to leave."

Nothing. Then when she spoke he strained to hear the soft words. "Very well."

Sharp and clear, the darkness faded to a dull, earthy dusk. He cried out as her scent left him, mint and jasmine fading into decades of spilled beer and old spunk. Gagging, he rushed to the bathroom as vomit shot up his esophagus, splattering the floor and sink before plopping into the dingy toilet. Bile burned his throat and tongue. Aches ravaged his bones, seared his mind, and drained him of purpose until only a tiny spark remained—the final ember of a dying star.

His ember, not hers. Meager, mortal talent.

Pulling himself up, he wiped the stinging mess from his lips, and washed his hands, then shuffled to the dresser. The next album would be his, with just a hint of Polyhymnia for inspiration.

Staring down at the open drawer, a moan escaped his throat. Page after page of sheet music lay in disordered piles, smudged and smeared beyond readability. He rushed to his laptop, typed in his username, and hesitated.

To log in he needed the password, the same word he'd used for everything—all his notes, his music, his output for the past two years—and in his mind her memory burned in its place.

"No." He tried a guess, something from his childhood. "No!" Another, the name of his first kiss. Her sad laughter mocked him, though real or imagined he couldn't say. "No!"

He breathed in, then out, forcing calm, drawing from his own strength, the strength he hadn't had to use in years. The memory came, and he typed, hit enter.

The first file wouldn't open, corrupted beyond recovery. And the second, and the third. All of them. Hammering at the keys, he checked the cloud. Gone, every note, every lyric.

He threw the machine against the wall, shattering it to pieces.

Fingernails raked at his scalp beneath his hair. She'd taken everything. Not only everything they would have done but everything they had. Every note, every lyric, every spark of passion and energy he'd channeled over two years.

His own spark flickered, defiant against the darkness, and he gritted his teeth. He could do this, would do this, without her. Without anyone.

"Dominic!"

Ken's voice reverberated through Dominic's skull, an unwelcome reminder that consciousness exists.

He opened his eyes, ran his tongue across gritty teeth tasting of cheap beer and cheaper girls, one of whom slept next to him on her stomach, naked except for a Deathsmack T-shirt that didn't quite hide the lumpy tramp stamp of "Cindy" in faded blue-black.

She snored, her breath a fetid mix of rotting garbage and margarita, chest rising and falling over the mound of belly fat spilling out across his mattress.

"Dominic!"

Clambering over Cindy, he struggled on a pair of dirty boxer shorts and called up the stairs. "What, dude, what? Christ, you don't have to yell!"

In a forced, calmer tone Ken continued. "I didn't want to walk in on nothing, and you didn't respond the first couple times."

"All right, all right, I'm awake." He shuffled up the stairs into the kitchen of their shared apartment, where faded linoleum and peeling paint served as a constant reminder that time consumes all things.

Ken leaned against the stove, a doobie hanging from his lips. "Put some clothes on, man, we got to go."

The ember cherry flared as he sucked in a drag. Ashes tumbled out across his chest. He held it, then breathed out a long stream of smoke. "Gig starts in an hour and we still have to set up. I'm going, so meet us there in ten minutes."

He still couldn't believe how quickly it had all disappeared. He'd left Deathsmack to set out on a solo career, financing his own album over the objections of his agent and band-mates. On his own without Nia and her "gift." Three years later, bankrupt and hitless, he begged them to take him back, to gig with them opening for newer, hotter bands. The look of pity—Pity!—on Ken's face had enraged him, but here he was, the glamorous life of a single-album has-been.

Almost thirty years old, living with his band-mate, drunk every day, drunker every night, he couldn't stomach another mall opening, hosting another Battle of the Bands, another out-of-town trip being some small-town bar's "special feature." But he had to eat, and Deathsmack paid his bills—he didn't know how to do anything else.

His mother's pastor's brother owned a landscaping company, and their grand reopening just had to have the local flavor of Deathsmack to rile up the crowd of graying simpletons before they stormed the gates for discounted bags of mulch. Hate coursed through him for his mother, his town, his band, his life. For Nia, who'd blessed and cursed him with the same casual sociopathy with which she'd taken and left her lovers. She'd shown him heaven just to let him fall into hell.

The band unloaded their gear and set up on the sidewalk to the left of the main entrance, just under a bright red awning. After a quick sound check he ducked under the ribbon across the front doors and inside, working his way across gleaming tile and past perfect shelves toward the sign that said "Restroom."

Mint and jasmine tickled his nose from the ajar door next to the men's room, a slice of pure black void against the industrial plastic tile wall. The world sharpened, a twisting memory wound through his head and dragged him toward it. The doorknob shocked him, protesting with a squeak as he turned it and stepped through into near-total darkness.

She sat in shadows on the desk, legs crossed, bare feet bobbing over discarded black stilettos.

"Hello, Dominic. How've you been?"

Hot rage seared his skull. "You know how I've been."

"I do, but it's polite to ask."

A growl escaped his throat. "You ruined me."

"You had forty million fans at twenty-two. You ruined you when you rejected me."

"I had no fans. You had fans."

"You still have no fans, only now you have no money and no fame, frittered away on cocaine and beer and bar sluts unworthy of the old names that grace their lower backs." She chuckled, then, as the lights in the hall flickered and dimmed. "Oh, the arrogance of mortals. Do you think you were the first to think you were different? Special? That your star would shine so bright without mine?"

She blazed, becoming a white inferno that scoured him to individual atoms, blasting him into plasma forged in a living sun. Her voice exploded around him; a wordless, godless, eternal reminder of the insignificance of man. The furnace of her existence raged through him, devoured him, forged and remade him, the quintessence of his every desire trapped in human flesh—and then it fell back to nothing but a glimpse, a promise, a lie. And then, a spoken truth.

"It's not too late, Dom. We can *be* again, and all that I am can be yours. Just let me in."

He picked himself up from the floor, a line of drool trickling from his mouth, and met her gaze. In them, glory blazed. "I want that. I want to be what you can make me."

"No barriers this time. I'll be within you, and you'll live as you always should have."

He nodded, humbled, exalted. Ready.

"I will."

She smiled, and faded to nothing.

He breathed in, out. "So that's it, then? We're ready?"

Her voice echoed within him. *I've been ready a long time.*

The priest looked up in alarm as Dominic shouldered the heavy wooden box through the door. His arm swept across the table to knock the tarot cards to the floor, spilling beeswax from black and red candles as they tumbled across the pentagram etched into the mahogany top. He sized Dominic up and down, then nodded to the chair under the crucifix, Christ's eyes upturned to a Father that had forsaken him.

"I know you."

Dominic nodded. "Everyone knows me, or knows of me. The price of fame."

"How may I help you?"

He licked his lips, swallowed, and sat, setting the heavy box on his lap. "I have an entity in my body struggling to take over, and it's become more difficult to control than I'd anticipated. I've been told you're the man to get rid of it."

"That may be. Explain your situation, please."

"There's nothing to explain. We've lived together three years, and it's outgrown its usefulness. We'd had a deal, it misunderstood, and I'm tired of fighting. I just need it gone."

The priest clucked his tongue. "I see. What is the entity? And do you know its name?"

She nodded Dominic's head. "His name is Dominic, and he's the human born to this body."

The priest smiled. "Did they tell you my price?"

Dominic wailed, silent in the void, as he'd wailed for three endless years.

She lifted the lid with a grunt, tilting the box so the priest could see within. Inside slept a two-year-old, her tiny body curled into a fetal position. She'd said her name was Alice, and that she wasn't supposed to talk to strangers, but took the lollipop anyway. Now deep in slumber, she drooled around a limp thumb stuffed between her lips. Cindy's child, Dominic's daughter, sired and abandoned the day Nia had taken him; she'd never seen a penny of child support, never a glimpse of her father's face except perhaps on posters or magazines.

The priest nodded, lust oozing from his eyes. "That will suffice. I'll get my knives."

Three hours later, the Star hopped aboard the tour bus, a grin splashed across its face to match those of its roadies and band-mates. "Time to make some music."

WELL WORN

Shelly tutted and muttered as she worked, as she'd tutted and muttered for fifty-odd years; an endless routine for an endless job. Grousing never changed the gone and done, but it suppressed decades of raw fury to a simmer.

Arthritic hands burned as she picked at the stitches. Forcing the seam ripper under the "E" embroidered on the red college varsity letterman jacket, she tore out dingy white threads and identity with every wobbly jerk.

"Girl, are you sure you want to do this again?" The shop's contents muffled her rheumy voice, tickled by a trace of Louisiana French that softened the consonants on the ends of her words. Shaky words, soft words, frailer with each autumn, but while the Pleiades ascended toward their highest point she knew her daughter could hear her.

Costumes smothered racks of old clothing and blocked most of her view, the other half of the store swallowed by masks and shoes and every kind of prop from plays and movies dating back a century and more. Shelly had sewn half the suits and nearly all the dresses on her grandmother's Singer, jet black with chipped and faded gold paint that may once have been a scroll, its original glory made plain by the ravages of time. Family legend said Old Nana had bought it two years after Lincoln's death with every penny she'd saved during twenty-four months of freedom, and brought it with her to New Orleans after the flood of 1882.

"It's not his fault, you know. Whoever he is."

Alice didn't reply; she never did.

Shelly tore out the rest of the stitches, sewed a rampant stallion patch in its place, and held up the candy-apple red garment. "It isn't maroon, cherie, but it'll have to do."

The brass bell on the door jangled as she put the jacket on the rack, where it hid in shadow to await the right customer.

Gail wrinkled her nose as the bell on the door faded to memory. Fluorescent bulbs in hanging cages bathed endless racks of vintage clothing in sickly, flickering light and added a sharp tang of over-heated wiring to the off-putting aroma of mothballs and must. Shelly's Costumes and Theater Supply smothered most of an out-of-business grocery store in aisle after aisle of vintage looks dating back more than a century.

Ball gowns of a bygone age hung on the back wall, pinks and blues and yellows protected from the ravages of sunlight by the blackened windows. Masks of every sort dominated the left-hand wall, classic movie monsters and smiling doll's faces to the creepy, long-faced plague masks from darker times. A mannequin stood to the right of the door, her headless, naked body bedecked in hundreds of necklaces, bracelets, anklets, and belly chains, "Costume Jewelry Priced as Marked" written across her outstretched arms in black marker.

Gail wandered back in time through the women's half of the room, past Cindi Lauper and Cher dresses, skipping pencil skirts and short-sleeve sweaters to pause at an emerald-green taffeta gown that screamed authentic Dior. A flapper's dress with a matching, sequined headband drew her onward, to a pile of whalebone corsets and enormous, antebellum wigs dumped in a heap next to an empty rack. A wig might be fun to cover her short black curls, something like a one-day weave, but there was no way she'd survive a shift at the hospital squeezed into Victorian-era garb.

"May I help you, child?"

"Oh!" Gail gasped, heart hammering as she turned to face the sudden voice. An old black woman smiled, thin lips cracking through a wall of wrinkles, her short afro a shock of dandelion fluff framing her walnut face. Hand flat against her chest, Gail forced a smile of her own. "You startled me. Sorry."

The old woman looked up at the racks, two feet higher than her head, then back to Gail. "Well, I do tend to blend in." Her eyes widened a smidge, which would have been welcoming if not for the bloody lines crackling across the edges of her sclera. "Theater or Halloween?"

Gail swallowed. "Neither, I guess." She laughed, bright and loud. "Or both. A Halloween party, but I'll be on my feet at work all day, a nurse, so nothing too …" She ran a finger across a corset, tracing across the butter yellow coutil to the whale bone under—

"Those were never for us, dearie, not back then."

Train of thought shattered, she stepped back, confused. "Us?"

Withered, shaking fingers took hers. The dry, papery skin almost brittle under her touch, long, thick nails yellowed by the passage of years. Yin and Yang, light and dark, white and black.

The old woman squeezed her palms, fingernails pricking just enough to hurt before letting go. "No need to pass with old Shelly. I know my people."

Gail felt a scowl forming and schooled her features to neutrality, her bedside face, her difficult patient face. "I'm not 'passing,' thank you. My mom was white, my dad is black. I don't hide my heritage."

Shelly smirked. "My husband was white. Quite the scandal in those days, even in New Orleans, a young man home from the war taking a seventeen-year-old French Quarter Negro to wife. But our daughter, see, she was a black girl. God rest them both."

"I … I'm sorry."

"Me, too." Shelly waved it off. "But that was a long time ago. What are you thinking for your costume?"

She set out down the row with a shrug. "I'm not sure. I guess I'll know it when I see it."

Behind her, Shelly's voice rose, both louder and lighter. "Well, if you need something I'll be around."

"Thanks!"

Gail browsed, and laughed out loud at a knee-length poodle skirt, powder blue with a black and white dog rolled on its back. The felt whispered to her fingertips as she picked it up, held it to her waist. It came just to her knees, a few stray threads dangling farther but in otherwise excellent shape for a sixty-year-old garment.

She grabbed a jet black mock-turtleneck, sleeveless and sleek, and a black-and-white polka-dot scarf trimmed in the same blue as the skirt. Turning, she called out. "Do you have a dressing room?"

"Back left," came the reply.

She changed, unable to suppress a manic grin at the sheer authenticity of the look, gave a twirl in front of the mirror, and stepped out.

Shelly put a shaking hand to her mouth. "Oh, how you look like her."

Gail's smile died in infancy. "Your daughter?"

Shelly nodded. "A beauty, right down to the green-flecked eyes."

Stepping back, Gail looked in the mirror. Her light brown eyes did look a little green, but only a touch. Must have been the lighting.

"How much?"

The old woman's eyes flicked from piece to piece. "Twenty dollars through Monday. No deposit, but ten a day after."

"Can't I just buy them?"

Shell's sad smile tore at Gail's heart. "Those were my Alice's. I can't let them go."

Gail opened her mouth, closed it, tried again. "I'm so sorry. I didn't—"

"No, no, of course you didn't. I wouldn't have them out if I didn't want people to wear them. They're yours for the weekend, for your discomfort."

"I couldn't." The thought of wearing Shelly's dead daughter's clothes shivered through her. They clung to her skin like a film of scum on a stagnant puddle.

The old woman's smile brightened.

"Come now, cherie, she'd want you to. I know it."

The feeling vanished, replaced by a sense of rightness, of purpose. The costume would give a mother peace … and it did look great on her.

"Then I'll take them for twenty."

In the end they settled for fifteen, Gail haggling up as the nonagenarian tried to undersell her own garments. She paid, changed back into her own clothes, and left the store.

Sunlight battered her down. Squinting, she walked to her car, skirting as far as she could get from the homeless white man drooling into his beard.

Passing. The shopkeeper's words followed her out.

She'd done it in high school, but not since growing into her own. College had taught her pride, in herself and her history. The accusation turned to bile in her throat.

Shelly frowned as the young woman disappeared around the corner.

"I'm so sorry." She looked up at nothing in particular. "Fifty years, cherie. Does it have to be fifty-one?"

Alice didn't answer; she never did.

An hour later the skies had turned to gloom, and distant thunder shook the windows. A fair-haired man in a T-shirt and jeans ducked inside, soaking wet, chest heaving. In response, the red jacket quivered on the rack.

"Look at him," she said. "Young, full of life and promise. That boy did nothing to you. You look at him and you tell me this is right."

Alice didn't answer; she never did.

Shelly closed her eyes, choking down a sob to replace it with a smile. She cleared her throat and raised her voice.

"Hello, young man! You look like you need something to keep the rain off."

"Damn straight, lady."

"Shelly, please."

His grin brightened the store and shattered her heart. "Dave. Charmed."

She pulled the jacket from the rack. "I have just the thing for this weather."

He looked at it, laughed as only the young can laugh. "Not really my style, but thanks."

"Please, take it." She pressed it into his hands. "I insist."

"Sure, Shelly. Got any umbrellas?"

She nodded to a rack on the prop side. "Just parasols."

He picked one up, bamboo, lemon yellow with creeping vines of wisteria, either Japanese or made to look like it. "How much?"

"Five bucks."

"Sold."

"Yesterday" by the Beatles warbled through the transistor radio on the vanity, softer and more poignant than their last hit single, and inescapable for the past six weeks. Alice twirled back and forth in front of the mirror, a grin plastered on her face. The powder blue poodle skirt and sleeveless black turtleneck showed off just enough dark brown skin to draw the eye, sexy and coy in the same breath. Not bad for six dollars.

Still, it needed something.

She pulled a polka-dot scarf from the closet, black and white, and tied it babushka-style over the curly riot of black hair on her head. The traces of green in her eyes popped, the most obvious touch of her father's legacy; Darryl would love it.

A throat cleared. She turned, smile already fading.

Beth stood in gray jersey pants and a white T-shirt, dark brown hair in pink curlers. Her roommate wore the shirt out on the town like servicemen home from the war, often without a bra, a scandalous bit of fashion Alice couldn't bring herself to imitate. Her mother had raised too much of a lady.

"Nice costume. Going Trick-or-Treating?" The accusation in Beth's tone sawed at Alice's mood.

"Very funny." Alice put on bright red lipstick and blotted it. "Darryl is taking me to the drive-in."

"You know that's not a good idea."

"I'll be fine." She crossed her arms. "What am I going to do, not date?"

"Not date a white boy, maybe. Or not in public. It's just asking for trouble."

A grin blossomed on her lips. "He is trouble, but the right kind. And times are changing, you'll see. Speaking of, guess what we're seeing?"

Beth rolled her eyes and walked out, then hollered back, "Something gross, I'm sure."

"*Monster of Terror*. Debuted Thursday. It's about—"

"A terrible monster, of course. Or some guy in a rubber suit. Sounds ridiculous. Just don't forget it's Sunday; you've got work tomorrow."

"Thanks, Mom." Sarcasm lingered after the words had escaped. Horror movies freaked Darryl out more than they did her, but she took the excuse to cuddle up against him either way, and if that led to a late night all the better. Worst case she could always call in sick.

Gail blotted her crimson lipstick and rubbed the waxy film from her front teeth. Scarf tied over her hair, eyelashes bold and long, a touch of foundation to smooth out the imperfections in her skin. And the old woman had been right—her eyes looked almost green from the right angle.

"Who are you tonight?"

She turned to her roommate, Amy, leaning against the doorframe in her boyfriend's Pantera T-shirt, large enough to cover a pavilion. With a carton of Ben & Jerry's Chunky Monkey in her left hand and a spoon in her right, Beth clearly had no plans to find a job, or go out at all.

"It's Halloween. I'm anyone I want to be."

Amy raised an eyebrow. "Dorothy Dandridge or Joan Crawford?"

"How about Grace Kelly?" She twirled, letting the skirt flare up past her knees, dancing in the high heels.

"In a poodle skirt?"

"Why not? It's a day of magic—anything can happen!"

"Which in this case is?"

"Work all day, stupid office party, then I'm catching a flick with Steve."

"What are you seeing?"

"Some stupid monster movie from the sixties."

"Ugh, have fun with that."

She smirked. "I don't think we'll be doing much watching."

"Gross."

Alice's high heels clopped down the sidewalk as the last October sun cast its final, long shadows between the rows of crumbling, postwar housing. Shrieks and giggles exploded to her right; a man in a white sheet chased a gaggle of children from his porch, bellowing and waving his arms. A little girl rode her pink bicycle across the grocery store parking lot, basket loaded with paper bags full of candy, her wide-brimmed witch's hat the perfect complement to the warty, green nose strapped across her face. The air smelled of cut grass and fallen leaves and an acrid hint of diesel exhaust from trucks on the new expressway roaring past town.

The orange-red glow of a cigarette illuminated eyes on the porch swing of a dark house, watching without blinking as Alice passed by. The ember died, and the eyes with them, darkness hiding the misshapen lump of the watcher's body, only to resurrect and die again.

Squeals of terror and joy mingled with the bite of cold air signaling the end of fall. The papers called for frost, and a hard freeze later in the week. More adult sounds filtered over the houses from the A&W on Wallen Street, laughter and hollering overtop the Juke Box blaring *Eve of Destruction* through speakers turned up too loud. A few brown leaves clung bitterly to naked branches, their cousins long since raked and carted off to mulch piles outside of town.

A shadow loomed, blocking the remains of dusk. A man.

He blocked her path, wife-beater stretched over his beer belly and around his sausage neck, frayed denim overalls stained with oil and grease. He sported a tattoo on his right bicep, a giant octopus entangling a Navy ship, *USS Downes* beneath it.

"You're in the wrong neighborhood."

She huddled around herself and stepped off the curb into the road. "I'm leaving, sir."

He shifted to get in front of her. She cut across the street and he followed.

"You're damned right you're leaving. We don't need your kind stinking up our streets, not even on Devil's Night."

She said nothing, walked faster.

"Hey! I'm talking to you!" Shoes flapping on pavement. Hot breath on the back of her neck. Rough hands grabbed her shoulders, cruel fingers digging into her skin, spinning her around to his hot breath in her face, garlic and onions and stale beer.

She cried out.

Dave ran his hands over the jacket, his Most Interesting Man in the World costume cast aside on the bed. Tina would be dressed as a bottle of Dos Equis, so the jacket didn't make a lot of sense.

The wool whispered against his fingertips, the leather sleeves smooth and cool to the touch. It pulled at him, cajoled him to put it on, strut around like the jock he'd never been.

His phone buzzed again, rattling itself off the dresser to the floor. Fog clouded his vision, turned his gaze back to the red fabric. He hadn't worn it since the storm, but had kept it in his closet just in case.

And didn't remember taking it out.

The stallion emblem galloped through his mind, drove him to put it on.

So he did, sighing as confused memories intruded on his brain; a sock hop at the school, staring at the girls from the lonely corner; seeing *her*, unable to summon the courage to approach; the pull of braided twine around his neck, feet kicking for a stool he couldn't reach.

Standing with the authority of purpose, he patted the inside pocket, pulled out a small box. An insulin kit with a tiny needle, treatment for a disease he didn't have. He tucked it back inside and stalked out the door. On the street he took a right, away from the suburbs and his girlfriend's party, away from the lights of downtown toward the Ward, a hot, mingled mess of college town and subsidized housing.

Purpose drove him, someone to meet, to own. She didn't know he existed, but after tonight he'd have her, and they'd be together forever.

Freshened up but not refreshed, Gail trotted down her apartment stairs as fast as the high heels would allow. A ten-minute turnaround had given her enough time to touch up her makeup and splash on some perfume—hibiscus and vanilla, Steve's favorite—but no time to sit and relax, to brush off a day of moaning patients and abusive, know-it-all doctors barking orders.

She reached her car, grabbed the door handle, and hesitated. A horn blared on the expressway, an impatient trucker punctuating that everyone had somewhere to be. Letting go of the handle, she turned, confused. An easy drive, a much longer walk. Walking to the theater would clear her mind, settle her mood before their date. And if she showed up five minutes late instead of her regular ten minutes early, Steve would understand.

Smoothing down the skirt, she leaned against the car, looked to the light-drowned stars to gather her thoughts.

Passing.

Nothing declared fearlessness like a walk through the white trash ghetto.

The high heels hindered her movement, forcing smaller, faster steps rather than an athlete's easy glide. Two blocks in she kicked them off and looped them through her purse strap. She'd dressed for an indoor party, not a long walk, and the cool air and colder concrete raised goosebumps across her exposed legs and arms. Removing the scarf from her head, she let it drape across her shoulders, lending meager warmth to the growing night.

Bass reverberated from a house flickering with strobes, dubstep or dance music indistinguishable through the shaking walls. A pair of men vaped next to the porch, sucking on their electric sticks through the mouth-holes in plastic werewolf masks. As she passed, they broke away from the porch, low, easy gaits just enough to keep from falling out of sight.

She sped up, glanced back. They kept pace.

The concrete abraded her feet, a continuous emery board rubbing skin raw. She gathered her skirt up, bundling the fabric in fists at mid-thigh, and fumbled for her phone. She held the power button and the boot up screen cast the inside of her tiny purse in a red glow. Three steps turned her walk into a run as she passed the grocery store, closed for the evening and dark except for the "No Loitering" sign.

Howls broke the air.

The phone flashed ready. She entered her code at a dead sprint, thumbed the phone icon.

Her head rang. Limbs tangled.

She'd run into someone at a full speed, knocking them both to the ground. Turning, she recoiled from his werewolf mask, and the hateful eyes behind it.

"How you doing?" he said, his lips an obscured blur behind a tiny slit.

She screamed.

Alice whirled and batted at the fat sailor's hands.

His fist stole her breath, knocked her stumbling onto the curb. Gagging, she rolled to her side, face against the grass.

Not the first time she'd been beaten, but the first since ninth grade. A gang of white boys had kicked and punched her not for daring to outperform them on an algebra test, but for doing so while black. They'd put her in the hospital, and not one had been arrested.

Streetlights faded as the sailor blocked the light.

"Told you, you don't belong here." He cracked his knuckles.

"Hey!" A dark shape slammed into her assailant and they disappeared from sight in a series of dull thuds and slapping noises.

She struggled to her hands and knees, raised her eyes.

Fists up, the men circled, one fat and at least forty, the other lean and young and vaguely familiar, face white under cheesy Boris Karloff vampire makeup that clashed with his maroon Stallions jacket. The vampire ducked a wild haymaker and jabbed the sailor in the nose. He stumbled back; the boy hit him again.

Arms up in a block, her attacker grinned through blood. "That all you got, pipsqueak?"

In a single smooth motion, the boy extended a hand. A knife sprang from the handle hidden in his palm; a switchblade. "Time for you to go home, old man."

His eyes flicked from the knife to the vampire's eyes, then back to the knife. Puffing his chest, he turned, calling out. "You're not worth my time."

A stumble up the porch steps ruined his bravado, and he slammed the front door behind him.

The knife disappeared. He turned to her, hand outstretched, cool as a cucumber. "Hi, I'm Tim. You want to blow this joint before he comes back with friends?"

Frowning, she studied his face, tried to drag a memory from the void of time. "Do I know you?"

He bobbed his head, something between a nod and a shake. "Sort of. I was a couple grades below you at Franklin Academy, but we never really met. You're Alice, yeah?"

"Yeah."

She took his hand, knuckles slick with the other man's blood, and he hauled her up.

Gail scrambled back on the ground to put some distance between her and the sailor—the wolf—she'd knocked down. Leaping up, she bolted, and the other wolf blocked her path, arms spread wide.

"Get away from me!"

His laugh sent a shudder up her spine. "You don't have nothing to worry about. We're just having a little fun."

We don't need your kind stinking up our streets, not even on Devil's Night. The thought stabbed through her, a jolt of electric, irrational hatred.

They circled.

A scream punctured the night, followed by laughter. In the distance a group of children yelled, "Trick or treat!"

"Scream if you want to," the first wolf said. "Adds to the fun."

Told you, you don't belong here.

They charged.

She dropped to her knees and delivered a one-two punch to the first guy's balls. He stumbled past, and the other jerked left to avoid him. She spun, shin catching the second man in the ankle. He fell to his back, rolled sideways just in time to avoid a chop to the throat.

As the boys dragged themselves up, she advanced, fists raised. They hesitated, ran, and she whirled at approaching footsteps.

"Hey!" A light-haired man slowed to a stop, his red varsity jacket emblazoned with a blue-and-gray stallion, eyes glazed, confusion etched across his rugged features.

She squared off, schooled her breathing, ready. "Back off, man."

"You're supposed—are … are you okay?"

She nodded. "I am. But I lost my phone back there and we need to call the police."

Patting his jeans, then his jacket, he frowned. "I don't have one."

"Are *you* okay?"

His eyebrows furrowed. "I'm not sure. I think so. Yes. Are you?"

He shied back as she stepped toward him, then shook her offered hand. Soft and smooth with a hint of calluses near the tip of his middle finger. A student's hands. Someone without a job.

"What's your name?"

"It's … Tim."

She grinned. "You sure?"

He swallowed, nodding. "I guess so."

"C'mon, let's find my phone, Tim. I'm Gail."

"Gail?"

"That's what I said."

"Huh."

His slow, sidelong glance up and down her body sent another

flurry of goosebumps across her arms. Way too many drugs in this neighborhood.

Tim sauntered with easy confidence, leading Alice between houses toward the center of town, his maroon jacket a beacon under the fading mercury lights. "Let's get you warm and see to that lip."

She hesitated. "I have a date."

His smile dazzled, as bright as his makeup. "I figured."

"Did you?"

His sidelong glance wormed across her curves. "Dolled up like that? You don't look like you're hunting Tootsie Rolls with the kids."

A grin crept to her lips. "I'm not. And you?"

"Me?"

"Yeah. What are you hunting?"

He chuckled. "Same thing as usual, I guess. Let's get you inside, then I'll give you a ride wherever you're going. You won't be late."

Five minutes later she sat at a dinette table, eyes tracing patterns across the linoleum floor as Tim put on the tea. He'd wiped his face with a towel, leaving streaks of white on his ears and cheeks between ruddy patches of skin, and his lips no longer matched his jacket.

"Thank you," she said for the hundredth time.

"It was nothing. Fat coconut thinks he can beat up a chick on my watch? He needed some learning. Still …"

"Still what?"

The kettle screamed. He poured them each a cup, set one in front of her—chamomile—along with a honey jar. She lifted the wooden honey dipper, drizzled a little into her cup, put it back. Fingers warmed by the near-boiling water, she smiled.

"Thank you."

"You need to stop saying that."

The tea soothed her throat, too sweet and almost too hot; perfect. She gulped it down, and he poured her another. "Maybe someday I'll stop, but my mom taught me gratitude. She'd do anything for me, and I've always been thankful."

"No, I mean, he had a point." Tim leaned on the table, hands flat, fingers splayed. "Girl like you in that neighborhood's just asking for trouble."

The honey turned bitter in her mouth. "A girl like me."

"Yeah. You need to be more careful." He glanced away, then back. "Look, I don't make the world; just live in it."

Her tongue turned thick with distaste. "No, I suppose you don't."

His hand flashed and a sharp prick stabbed her neck. She slapped at it, pushed back in her chair.

Struggling to get words out, she tried to raise her eyes from the syringe that clattered on the table. Too sluggish, too slow, and the world swam. By the time she'd looked up he'd circled behind her, fingertips brushing up her arms to her shoulders, electric and dull at the same time. She tried to lift her arms but they lay heavy at her sides. Her head lolled back, eyes rolled to meet his, staring down in rapture.

"We're going to be so wonderful together. I promise."

"What—"

A white-hot line tore across her throat. Coppery, meaty liquid filled her mouth and bubbled from her ruined neck. A kitchen knife clattered to the table, awash with bright red blood. Their eyes met in its reflection. She spasmed, choking, lungs aflame.

He leaned down and kissed her forehead, his shuddering sigh the pale shadow of her last wracking breaths.

"Thank you."

"No, no. This way." Tim grabbed Gail's hand, tugged her toward the side of the road.

She frowned at the black space between the driveway and the house, a patch of nothing but dark promises. "Why would we go that way?"

The glazed look in his eyes intensified. "'Cause that's the way, man. We'll get you cleaned up and warmed up and then you can get your phone and go on your date. I'll give you a ride wherever you're going. You won't be late. I … I promise."

She stepped back. "I don't need cleaning up. And how did you know I was going on a date?"

"You told … I mean … look how you're dressed, Alice!"

Another step back, hands raised, keeping him in view. "It's Gail. And hey, thanks for the heroics, but I'm going to get going. You have a nice night."

A pathetic cry escaped his throat. His eyes cast downward, tears brimming, and when he looked up they crackled with green. "We're going to be so wonderful together. I promise."

"Back off." She took another step, keeping him in sight.

He lunged, snarling. She deflected his clumsy chop down away from her neck, grimaced at a sharp stab to her thigh.

A palm-strike broke his fingers and shattered the hypodermic needle he'd buried in her muscle. Liquid splattered across the skirt. Glass dug into her skin, and burned.

Heat spread from the injection; the arteries in her neck throbbed. He advanced, she backpedaled. Too sluggish, too slow, and the world swam. Strong hands wrapped around her throat.

He squeezed.

She sucked in nothing, clawed at his wrists, fingernails scraping across red leather sleeves. A fury poured into her, filled her as oxygen wouldn't, overlaid Tim's face with another. Smoother, younger, crueler, smears of stark white makeup across his face, mouth open in rapture and want.

Harder.

Her head pulsed, and as she groped in vain at air that wouldn't come, shadows encroached the edges of her vision. She punched but couldn't build the momentum to hurt him.

Teeth gritted, he bounced her head off the building behind her. Again. Again.

Hands scrambling, she fumbled at his pockets, grabbed something oblong but not much bigger than a pencil. She thumbed a button, cut her finger on the extended blade, and thrust.

Once.

Twice.

A dozen times, and with each stab a shriek of elation ravaged her mind, scoured conscious thought clean with ice-cold rage.

Tim fell, hot dark rivers spurting from his chest and stomach.

She gasped, fell to her knees, worked her mouth to suck in precious, cool air. Tim gurgled, red bubbles foaming from his lips. His glazed expression faded to pain and confusion.

Darkness fell.

The brass bell on the door jangled, and freezing air swirled through the shop.

Shelly stifled a smile fifty years in the making. Her daughter's triumphant return rustled through the racks, jostled shoes and props and set the hanging lights to dancing. She finished adjusting the seam on a band uniform—the local high school would be performing *The Music Man* and their Harold Hill stood five-two—and then pushed it aside as her customer shuffled around the corner.

In a full turtleneck obviously intended to hide the bruising, Gail hugged a brown parcel tied with twine. Dark bags lurked under her eyes, and a haggard ponytail released more wiry outliers than it contained. Her cheeks sagged, a side-effect of Tim's—Dave's—paralytic, poison Shelly had put in the jacket pocket before giving it to Dave. That haggard look would fade eventually, in weeks or months, maybe years. Green flecked her irises, flat and skittish, a scar that might never heal, not in this life.

Yet here she stood, beaten, battered, but alive.

"Hi, Shelly. Um, I'm sorry this is so late." Her confidence had vanished, replaced with a weary, wary resignation. She set down the package and fumbled for her purse. "What do I owe you?"

The old woman shook her head. No price could hope to match her daughter's soul returned, whole and hale, by the woman doomed to be a victim. "Nothing, cherie. I saw the news, saw what that boy did, what you had to do. I figure you paid enough for that night, and couldn't dream of asking for more."

Gail hung her head. "Thank you."

"Who was he?" Shelly couldn't help herself; she didn't want to know, but had to.

She looked at the floor. "Some guy from the neighborhood. Called himself Tim, but the cops identified him as Dave Taylor. His girlfriend visited me in the—you know, I'm just tired of talking about it, sorry."

"My apologies. That must have been hard."

Awkward silence reigned until Shelly's guilt filled it.

"Is there anything more I can do for you?" She couldn't beg forgiveness, and it took every ounce of willpower to hide her elation.

"No. Thank you."

"You don't have to keep saying that."

"I know." Gail turned without another word and shuffled back the way she'd come.

After the bell jangled again, Shelly waited, then reached up with quivering hands to tug at the string, each movement an effort grown harder with every passing day. With a bit of fuss the knot came loose and the paper uncurled, a flower greeting sunlight, to reveal her daughter's last outfit. The shirt and scarf almost looked new, but the skirt had faded another shade. A new hole, no bigger than the head of a quilt pin, frayed where the dry cleaner must have scrubbed blood from the felt. Threads weakened by the paralytic couldn't take that kind of abuse, so another shred of her daughter had fallen to nothing at a stranger's hands.

Her heart soared as she bunched up the clothing and slid it to the edge of the table, just over the waiting wastebasket.

"Finally. You've beaten him. She's beaten him." She sat up straight for the first time in decades. "It's done."

Alice didn't reply; she never did.

"No, daughter. You can't just … you can't. It's over. He's gone. You can rest now. I can rest now. It's time to let go."

"Please."

Alice didn't reply; she never did.

Her shoulders slumped. As she mended the skirt, she tutted and muttered, as she'd tutted and muttered for fifty-odd years; an endless routine for an endless job. Gripping the table, she forced her aching knees to support her weight and carried her daughter to the rack.

"Well whoever you wear next year, try to be kind."

TROPHY HUNT

The brick walls kept them out, and even with no fire they wouldn't dare come down the chimney; the prey had learned something from children's tales, but so had the hunters. Outside under the blazing sun their howls, shrill and unnatural, mingled with gunfire and raucous laughter. Their prey trapped, the hunt had become a party.

She stepped away from the door, the crack too small to see outside anyway.

"Beth."

She turned at her husband's voice, traced up his work boots and denim overalls to his rugged, angular face, just visible in the darkness. Her heart broke at the despair in his expression.

"They're going to get in."

She shook her head, an impotent denial of the inevitable. They'd taken the forest, she knew that. The game had fled or been slaughtered and devoured by the savages outside, no match for the trucks and ATVs and guns they'd taken to in modern day. Even rodents had gotten scarce, what trails there were crisscrossed and obscured by flat, wide tracks that stank of rubber and gasoline.

"No, baby, they're not. They're going to drink and fight and get tired and lazy, and we'll slip out when they don't expect it. This isn't a siege, it's—"

Creosote fell into the fireplace. Dust rained from the rafters. The floor shuddered as massive diesel engines rumbled in the distance.

"They're going to get in."

Her heart raged against the truth in it. The last of their kind, at least this side of the Rocky Mountains, they were too big a prize to let get away. *Homo sapiens sapiens* didn't brook competition. They never had, even after their scientists had learned that their myths were wrong, that their respective species couldn't crossbreed. If anything it had emboldened them, given them an endgame.

Bullets pecked at the façade, a waste of ammo and effort. Someone whooped in drunken triumph. More laughter, more whoops and hollering. More pecks.

Hunting them below population viability, dooming their species, that hadn't satisfied them. No, their bloodlust demanded lives, pelts, taxidermy bodies posed as fearsome statues by cabin fireplaces.

Bragging rights. The scourge of the darkness under the pines, the masters of night, the lords of the moon; their hunters had reduced them to not only to prey, but to bragging rights.

God, how she hated them.

The house shuddered again.

The hatred bloomed in her breast, spread through her in shockwaves, and she grunted at the first twinge of the change. She crouched, breaths short and shallow. Coarse brown hair sprouted from her arms, claws from her fingertips.

Strong hands grabbed her head, pulled her upright. She snarled and tried to back away, but John pressed her against the wall and locked her eyes with his. "No, baby, you can't do this. Not now. They want this. Want *us*."

She growled, deep in her throat … and he licked her cheek. Her cheek, her forehead, her hair. He held her and she folded into his warmth and let his words roll over her, soft babbled truths about love and hard lies about survival. He smelled of wolf and fear and desperation, of love and comfort and worry. She let the change bleed out of her and sighed, exhausted.

Thunder-that-wasn't rumbled in the distance, and she ran her fingers down his cheek.

"Thank you." They stood in silence a moment, but she couldn't help herself. "What do you think they're doing?"

"Felling trees. They're either going to make a battering ram or a giant bonfire."

They'd never get through the windows. The fort house had once been a frontier jail, and had thick iron bars in front of the glass, rusted and pitted with age but still thick. Behind them they'd nailed up thick hardwood boards and old tin sheeting. The hunters had tried to force the door, but the heavy steel held, and she'd shot three men through the mail slot to deter further attempts. She smelled them outside, the bloody bodies left as bait, but she couldn't risk opening the door. But God how she wanted to.

The hunters didn't know the wolves only had seven rounds left for the .308, the only reason they hadn't stormed the place.

She pushed him back with her fingertips, no longer claws. "Not a bonfire. They don't just want us dead, they want trophies."

"But they're cowards. If they breach the door or the wall, they know they're going to die. The first however many, anyway. They'll burn us out, just as soon as they're ready."

"No, baby, you're stuck in last century." Two centuries ago, really, but this one hadn't lost its baby teeth, at least in her mind. "They'll use grenades. A small hole, in it goes, and we're diving for cover or dead. They'll breach two places at once, split us up." She looked down, and wished she hadn't.

Their six pups dozed in the plastic laundry basket, heaped amongst dirty clothes and an old leather saddlebag, oblivious to the danger of their situation. Ears flat, they wouldn't open their eyes for another few days. Beautiful, fragile, helpless.

She hadn't eaten in two days, and hunger clawed at her ribs. The pups took from her what they needed and left her starving, and in a lean spring she'd be happy to give it. A pathetic cry tore at her heart, so she shifted, her once-sleek fur patchy with mange and malnutrition as she slipped from her human clothes. She tipped the basket and let her pups nuzzle against her, let them suckle. Weak from fear and starvation, she closed her eyes, head resting on the floor.

She didn't expect sleep to come, but pretending helped.

John waited for the sun to drop below the horizon before peeling back the board from the second story bathroom window. Campfires dotted the surrounding woodland, devoid of brush or cover. Scents of roasting meat and beer and piss filled his nostrils, but his dry mouth wouldn't salivate. They'd cut the power, and with it the plumbing, and what little water they had left would go to Beth. For the pups.

He waited and watched, his human eyes more suitable for long-distance scanning than his wolf eyes, despite the darkness. A man sat on a log not far off, binoculars in his lap, a sandwich in his hands. He didn't so much look at the house as stare off into space in that general direction. A bullhorn leaned against his ankle.

Lightning flashed in the distance, and John caught a glint next to a haggard beechnut tree. He waited and watched, and in time the silhouette resolved itself into a prone man or woman with a rifle, scanning the house through a scope.

He ducked back, replaced the board, and licked his lips. He'd seen two. How many more? How careful were they being?

The bloody, furry mess in the bathtub wouldn't answer him. Chet had taken a bullet in the chest, and while he'd made it into the house, it didn't take more than a minute for him to bleed out right through the bandage. At least it was too cold for flies.

John's stomach growled, and he turned away from the corpse. That path led to madness, and while his stomach didn't care, his mind still did.

They never should have come back for the pups.

Hayden looked up from the rifle, frowning. She'd expected another monster like she'd seen with her daddy, not a tired-looking man in overalls. He'd looked sad, worried, not hateful and violent. Not like a demon at all.

"The land ain't tame," Daddy had said. "Won't be, until the last of the monsters are gone."

Most people didn't believe in monsters. Her friend's parents taught them they weren't real. Her daddy had done the opposite, taught her and trained her, took her hunting and tracking from the time she could walk. And two weeks ago, for her fourteenth birthday, he'd given her a Ruger M77 .270 with a night-vision scope, and a trip to a "hunting safari" in western Montana.

Twenty men hunting five werewolves. It didn't seem fair.

The forward group harvested two before Hayden had even gotten into the truck, and the next few hours consisted of a harrowing chase through half-cleared woodland, bouncing over roots and creeks while her daddy lectured her on the technique.

"Like wolves'll run deer until they drop from exhaustion, you keep the weres on the run long enough and they'll turn and fight. They got way more endurance than you or me, but can't out-marathon a tank of gas.

"You hunt wolves like they hunt deer, not how we do."

They'd spotted their quarry just as they ran for a two-story brick fortress. Daddy'd fishtailed to a stop, and Hayden used the window as a bench rest. Huge beasts covered in dense fur, they moved so fast she had a hard time picking out detail. Humanoid, anyway, which told her all she needed to know. She'd trained on the front one, pulled the trigger just as he opened the door. His companions dove into him, carrying him through into the darkness.

"Dammit, Hay!" her dad had said as the door slammed shut.

"I got him." They locked eyes, but she wouldn't back down. "Solid shot, upper ribs. He won't make it."

He'd mussed her hair. "That's my girl."

Beth startled awake as a thunderclap rocked the building. John stood over her, human and dressed. "We need to go."

"What?" She sat up, naked and human, her pups mewling as they slid into her lap.

"They've got sentries, but the lightning'll blind them, and if the rain's hard enough it'll bog down their trucks."

She stood and pulled on her jeans, filthy denim covering legs clammy with old sweat. "They'll be watching the doors."

He nodded. "And the windows."

"So—"

He held up a finger to stop her, then pointed at the fireplace. "We go up."

She blinked in disbelief. "That's crazy."

"If we stay here we die."

She crouched, picked up her pups one by one and put them in the saddle bags. They didn't even have names yet, wouldn't until they were old enough to go on hunts with the pack—with their father, all that was left of their pack. Done, she pulled on a T-shirt and stood.

"Okay." Another peal of thunder rumbled through.

She crouched into the fireplace, rank with old soot, bat guano, and mold. Rain spattered her face as she looked up the chimney. Dark clouds blanketed the sky above the narrow opening, and claustrophobia tightened her chest. Wolves weren't meant for narrow brick crevices, weren't meant to climb.

She stood, just able to fit inside, and John cinched the saddle bags to her thigh.

"Go, baby. I'll meet you up top."

She pressed her forearms against the opposite side of the chimney and braced her back against the opposite wall. Her legs barely fit, and she dug her bare feet into the slippery gunk to keep any kind of purchase. John pushed from below to help her the first several feet, and a flood of lightheadedness struck the moment he let go.

"I can't—"

The saddle bags tugged at her leg, and she killed the excuse mid-breath. Her muscles screamed as she struggled upward, inch by agonizing inch, dragging her pups with her. Slick with ancient grime, she could barely move one limb while supporting herself with the other three. Below her, John inched upward, supporting the saddle bags and their precious cargo with his shoulders.

Lightning flashed, and thunder slammed the breath from her lungs. She wanted to rest, to stop, to give up, but had nowhere to go. So she climbed. And climbed and climbed. Halfway up, John swore, and the rifle clattered to the bottom.

"Leave it," she said.

He chuckled, a harsh sound devoid of humor. "Planned on it."

For an eternity she played Sisyphus. Muscles locked, even a rest gave no rest, and the higher she climbed the worse the rain slicked her arms, legs, and the soot-covered brick. The space crushed her, squeezed her lungs, strangled her rational thoughts and left her chained in a cage. Thunder rumbled, lightning flashed, revealing John below, murmuring words of encouragement and comfort, though to her or the pups or himself she couldn't hear.

At last the sky broke above her, and she grasped the edge of the chimney with a cry of despair just abated. Tears lost in the downpour, she hauled herself out and then lay flat on the cold slate roof, saddle bags clutched in her arms. The pups whined and yelped, and she prayed the rain would drown out their feeble protests.

John dropped next to her and they lay there, frozen in place in the deluge, for several minutes. She knew she had to move again, but wanted to close her eyes in the rain and let it wash her away into nothing. Her shredded muscles couldn't compete with the agony in her gut, the fire in her chest. But the sky, oh, how she'd missed the sky. Under the sky, in the rain, she could die happy.

"I can't do this," John muttered.

Anger fueled her, anger that he'd abandon her, that he'd give up on their pups. "You can. You will, dammit. We'll—" She caught his smirk in the lightning flash and wanted to kiss and kill him. "You son of a bitch, you got me."

As adrenaline sparked by anger burned through her, he smiled. "Next flash, to the edge."

She nodded, and tensed.

The sky lit and she rolled, arms tight around their precious bundle. She hit the wrought iron spikes on the edge of the roof and froze. Another flash, and she hauled over them, hung down as far as she could, and dropped.

Her stomach lurched. A tree exploded in a flash of white on a nearby hill. She hit the ground and cried out as her foot slid, wrenching her calf. Red-hot pain seared up her leg to her lower back, worse with every limping step to the shelter of the tool shed. John appeared beside her, and took their children from her arms.

Laughter and music rang out around them, the torrential downpour doing little to depress the spirits of their hunters. In every direction, campfires fought the rain, but no cries of alarm came from them.

"Are you all right?"

She shook her head, and kept her voice as low as his. "Landed funny. Hurts to walk."

"Okay. I'll help you." She shifted much of her weight onto his shoulders, and took a cautious step. "We'll go right through them. Just act naturally."

"No."

They whirled at the high-pitched voice, and John snarled.

A blonde girl stood not ten feet away, rifle slung across her back, hands empty and outstretched, palms up. Her ponytail stuck out from a Bass Pro baseball cap, and the water rolled off of her camo hunting suit. "Go South. Bill and Derek are drunk. I'll lead you."

John looked at Beth, deferring to the alpha female. Beth pressed her hand into his back, toward the girl. John stepped, she followed.

The girl smiled, pretty white teeth in perfect rows. "I'm Hayden. This way."

Beth grabbed her shoulder. "Why are you helping us?"

She shrugged. "My dad says you're monsters. You don't look like monsters to me."

They passed an unconscious man lying in a pile of beer cans. Beth snatched up his shotgun on the way by. Double-barreled, with six rounds tucked into a Velcro-and-elastic holder on the butt stock, it weighed a zillion pounds. She put it over her shoulder without complaint and plodded through the mud between the child and her husband, gritting her teeth against the pain in her ankle.

They walked for twenty minutes, then forty, stopping at a small creek to drink and fill Hayden's water bottle. The girl picked her way with easy assurance, one foot in front of the other without hesitation or even a hint of nervousness, every once in a while stopping to check a GPS she kept in her pocket. She glanced more than once at Beth's limp, but said nothing.

Another ten minutes and Beth stopped, set the shotgun in the dirt. "Wait, please."

They stopped. Beth smelled the wariness boiling off John, the jumbled discomfort of her pups.

Hayden smelled like soap and sweat and hot, bloody meat. She put her fists on her hips, an almost comical gesture in the pouring rain. "It ain't much farther." A pup whined, and Hayden looked at the bag. "Y'all got kids?"

John blinked. "Pups. Six. We need to get them to safety so they can nurse."

Beth hung her head, almost unable to speak. "I need food. Painkillers. I can't keep doing this."

Hayden smiled. "Safety's just around the corner."

"Where are we going?" John's voice projected distrust edged with contained hostility.

"A hunting cabin. The whole crew's supposed to meet up there tomorrow. After … after you're dead." She turned and walked, forcing them to lose her or catch up. They stumbled after her. Sure enough, they rounded an outcropping and in the distance saw a small cabin with a wrap-around porch, a single naked bulb shining out through the front window.

Beth cleared her throat. "And no one's there now?"

"Nope." Did she hesitate? Just for a split second? "They're all staking out your fortress. Plan to go in at sunrise, take you down. Hurry up!"

She took off at a jog.

Beth looked at John, read the desperate hunger there, felt it herself. She nodded. "Yeah."

He handed her the saddle bags on his way past. By his third step he'd changed, a seven-foot wall of sleek muscle, claws and teeth. He snarled as he leapt. Drool rolled down Beth's chin, and she almost fainted at the thought of fresh meat.

Hayden dropped prone, and John fell on top of her. He didn't catch himself, didn't land on his feet. Then Beth heard the shot, sharp and crisp.

She screamed.

Hayden grunted as the dead weight blasted the air from her lungs. Gushing liquid, so much warmer than the rain, ran down her face and hands, filling her mouth with the taste of iron and meat. The creature's musky scent overpowered the rotting leaves and new grass, and its thick fur almost blocked out the woman's scream.

A shotgun blast rang out. A rifle responded as she wriggled her way out from under the massive frame. Heavy footsteps stopped just behind her, and she rolled to her hands and knees and took the offered hand, rough with callouses and so, so strong.

Her dad hauled her to her feet.

"Did I do good, Daddy?"

He spat, a brown squirt of tobacco juice that disappeared into the carpet of dead leaves. "Yep. That male'll fetch us fifty grand, give or take. And ain't nobody else needs to know we got him."

"What about the female? She had pups."

He raised an eyebrow. "Pups, now? That's interesting."

"Six of them. Why interesting?"

He spat again. "I know a man's got a preserve up Ottawa way. You raise those pups right, you got one hell of a hunt in a few years." He took off her cap and rubbed her head, freeing strands of hair stained a muddy red-brown. "She's limping, and armed. You catch her, the pups are yours."

Hayden grinned, unslung her rifle and dashed after her prey.

THE EXTERMINATION BUSINESS

1

It was a Dark and Stormy kind of night, and I'd had four by the time the dame walked into my office. You know the deal: black dress, red lipstick, half a cigarette hanging from her mouth. Thing is, she couldn't pull it off. You ever scratch your ass and get more than you bargained for? Yeah, she looked like that.

"Mister Szymanski?"

"S'what the door says, toots."

Fatter than my ex-wife and twice as pretty, she tossed an envelope on my desk,

"I have a rat problem."

Yeah, the extermination business ain't glamorous, but it keeps the lights on.

2

I picked up the envelope, flipped through the bills. Twenties, a hundred of them, give or take. Smart girl. Even a dame doesn't come to Mike Szymanski short.

"Where?" I said, eyeing her up and down.

Something about her seemed so familiar, like I'd seen her at a Bat Mitzvah plowing through the rugelach, or behind the dumpster at Eddie's doing favors for the local flavor. Nothing wholesome, nothing nice.

"You know the apartments off Loyola?"

"Sure." I wouldn't call them "apartments" so much as a warren, one of those high-rise projects the cops avoid if they know what's good for 'em. Good way to get eaten. "Lots of rats in a place like that. What's a broad like you care about it?"

"They took my brother. He's only twelve."

"When?"

"Yesterday."

No way the boy was alive, but no use telling her that.

I shoved the envelope in the back of my pants, scooped my gun off the desk and stuck it in the holster under my flask. On second thought, I stuffed an extra handful of silver bullets in my pocket.

Wererats. I fucking hate 'em.

3

I followed her down the stairs, silver bullets jangling in my pocket.

"I'm Mindy, by the way." She took one last drag and flipped her cigarette butt into the gutter as we exited into the tiny parking lot. Four spaces, three empty, the last occupied by my rusty white panel van circa Johnny Carson was still on the air. "Michael Szymanski, Exterminator" stood out in touched-up green on the side over a painting of a legs-up roach with exes for eyes.

"Where's your ride?" I asked.

"My boyfriend dropped me off. Figured I could ride with you."

I paused, ran my tongue over my teeth for effect. "Did he, now?"

She nodded.

"What if I didn't take the job?"

"We knew you would. 'Sides, the check cleared."

I spat. "All right. Hop in."

She got in the passenger's side after I unlocked it, and we got on the road. By the time we hit Rangel Avenue, her funk had invaded my nostrils and was taking hostages; cigarette smoke and unwashed hair, body spray too manly—probably her boyfriend's—and a musty, farty something that reminded me of a guinea pig cage that hadn't been cleaned in too long.

The beat-up coup three cars behind us switched lanes when I did, twice. Put on my blinker for the wrong exit, and so did it, then we both drove on past.

"So," I said. "We going to do this here, or wait 'til we get there?"

4

She stared at me, the kind of stare you get from a disgruntled cashier when you try to be funny. And they're all disgruntled—just buy your crap and get out of the way.

I made a show of putting on my seatbelt, then snuck my gun out of the holster left-handed.

I don't know what went through her head at that moment. I'd like to think it was good thoughts, maybe about her boyfriend if he was real, about her kids if she had any, puppy dogs and butterflies or something. Something better than what would go through it later.

When those big buck teeth sank into my arm, I swung the pistol toward her morphing body and pulled the trigger, twice. I expected the transformation, the elongating skull, the wiry fur sprouting from her everywhere, even the ferocity and speed of the attack. But I hadn't expected her to jerk the wheel.

We served hard, skidded sideways at seventy miles an hour, and with a gun in one hand and a giant rat-faced psycho gnawing on the other, we hit the curb, hard. The van flipped, rolled, her teeth still savaging my arm and still growing. All of which totally would have been survivable if we didn't flip right over the overpass railing and into the traffic below.

Timing is everything, I guess.

5

My van crashed into the asphalt with a sickening crunch, staving in the passenger side and throwing Mindy or Linda or whatever her name was right on top of me. Addled and shell-shocked, for a second neither of us did anything but stare and wrangle up our ability to think.

She'd gone full rat by then, six feet long, lean and wiry and bloody-mouthed, and her breath was like getting slapped in the face with a sweaty wrestler's hairy armpit. I put my gun under her chin, only I no longer held it—like everything else in my van, it had become so much flotsam.

So instead, I pushed, pinning her head against the ceiling long enough to undo my seat-belt. She scratched and clawed at my arms, and her back legs shredded my shirt and made mincemeat of my stomach.

I'd just about started to get angry when a wailing horn and the screech of air brakes announced the arrival of a speeding tractor trailer with no room to swerve.

It obliterated my van, the dame, and me, smeared us across several hundred feet of highway in a red-brown streak of blood and gasoline.

And that really pissed me off.

6

I rose up from the cold metal slab and shook to clear the cobwebs from my brain. Or at least to get the spiders off 'em.

Looking down, I couldn't help but notice the clean boxers, simple black cotton with bright yellow smiley faces on them, like a too-cheerful Batman.

The baby-faced coroner stood over another body—Mindy—chest cut open to put each flabby breast face-down on either side, organs in a tray on another table. Her face still sported a good chunk of charred fur, and her incisors hadn't retracted. He dictated another sentence and then switched off the recorder as I hopped down.

"Hey, Mike." He jerked his head to indicate a plastic bag by the door. "Your stuff's over there."

"Did you put these on me?"

He grinned. "No, Sheila did."

"You know I hate it when you guys dress me."

Dave shrugged. "Wasn't much to dress. We had to play a little 'leg bone connected to the shin bone.'"

I shuffled across the cold floor and looked down at her.

"So what gives?"

He shrugged again. "The accident drove her right shoulder through her skull. Looks like someone shot her in the right shoulder with a silver bullet, so it proved fatal. Know anything about that?"

"How could I know anything? I wasn't even here."

I grabbed my stuff on the way out the door.

"See ya next time."

7

Zofia Szymanski was the kind of woman who would loan a cup of sugar to a neighbor, then give them shit about it for the next thirty-seven years. I couldn't quite say that, because Bob died at year thirty-six-and-a-half, probably from regret that his ex-wife borrowed a cup of sugar from my mom thirty-six-and-a-half years earlier.

"What are ya talkin' about, ya need to borrow the car? And what are ya doin' in your underwears?"

I pushed past her into the apartment—not much more than a shoe box with a giant plasma TV. Mom grunted in annoyance but let me through, hobbling after me on her walker as I helped myself to the bottle of scotch on the table.

Duncan's Dew. The perfect blend for stripping graffiti from bathroom stalls.

I poured two fingers and swallowed them, savoring the burn in my stomach and shuddering at the taste of peat and burnt hair aged in urine barrels.

"My van got totaled, Ma."

She grunted as I slapped her hand away from the smiley-face boxers.

"That was you that died last night?"

I sighed at the rhetorical question and the muttered Polish blessings and blasphemies that followed, and poured myself another double.

"Can I borrow the car or not? I have a job to do."

"Sure, Mikey," she said. "Take the Benz. But don't scratch it."

8

A jet black 1971 Mercedes-Benz W108 should have been a classic car, especially with a single owner over all of those almost fifty years, but the two things no machine can hold out against are entropy and Zofia Szymanski. I opened the creaking door and slid inside, the cracks in the leather seats catching at my leg hair as my ass shoved aside a McDonald's bag smeared with moldy ketchup. It didn't quite latch when I closed it so I opened it again and slammed it hard. Ancient upholstery rained on me from the ceiling.

Mom groused out the window at the rough treatment. I ignored her. She loved this damned car so much she'd have breast-fed it if she could have.

At least the engine sputtered to life on the third try.

I backed out of the drive and headed to the office—there wasn't much chance they'd be looking for me there, what with my being dead and all, but maybe they knew something most people didn't. So just to be careful I popped the glove box and pulled out mom's Taurus 454 Raging Bull. One of the original five-rounders, the revolver sported a 2.25" barrel, a hair trigger, weighed a ton, and kicked like a mule. Each slug had been made special, lead for weight, silver for trouble, blessed and benedicted and danced over by priests and rabbis and imams and shamans just for good measure. The hollow-points had been filled with gelatinized holy water.

In this line of work you couldn't be too careful.

9

I walked up the stairs, revolver in hand, and rolled my eyes when I got to the second-floor landing. My door lay ajar, glass shattered, safety screening torn through. The hall lay silent, but my nose told me they'd left me a surprise.

Great.

I stepped inside to a catastrophe. Laptop smashed to pieces, desk contents scattered, filing cabinets overturned with the papers scattered everywhere. Whatever they'd been looking for, they didn't find—all this crap was just for show, to make it look like I dealt with bees and ants and things, fifteen years of paperwork for jobs never done, invoices never paid.

Extermination was a cash business.

You ever seen a mouse turd? They're shaped like an elongated football about the size of a grain of rice, brown-black, real solid. Wererat turds are much the same, only the size of your thumb. This explained the thumb-sized football shapes on my desk, floor, and paper-piles. Stupid.

I leaned over one, breathed in real deep, let the body-processed fast food and dumpster garbage fill my nostrils. All things considered, it wasn't quite as bad as Duncan's Dew. I sampled a few more, careful not to touch them.

And now I had two clues: the scent of three rats, and a dark, beat-up coup, license plate STS-3951. Shouldn't be too hard to find.

Now I needed some clothes.

10

The extermination business has certain hazards. And I'm not just talking about careening off an overpass into traffic while some crazy broad is chewing your arm off. Turns out people don't much like getting killed, and tend to take it personally. That whole "it's not personal, it's business" thing is for the movies, and having a home address isn't a great idea.

So Mike Symanski's apartment isn't rented out to Mike Symanski, it's rented out to Chris Picknett. Chris is the best kind of roommate—dead. He doesn't eat much and keeps the vermin out, and doesn't have the corporeality to be much more than an amusement. He flicks the lights and rattles the cupboards now and then because he doesn't like company, especially when that company shot him in the face fifteen years earlier.

Don't worry, he deserved it.

After making sure I wasn't tailed, I made it home, took a nice long shower to wash off the disinfectant from the morgue and made myself the breakfast of champions—a Pop Tart and a half-dozen cigarettes. Chris unplugged the toaster halfway through, so I ate them luke-warm.

Any excuse for a party.

11

Now you might expect me to have some beat-up desktop computer, with a big, chunky monitor circa 1995. It fits the stereotype, sure, but the demands of my work require something with a little more oomph.

In 2009 I traded my iPad, twelve thousand dollars, and a phial of a virgin princess's tears for a sleek, black machine of unknown provenance. You know how a genie in a bottle will grant wishes in exchange for its freedom? Well, it turns out that an Ifrit in a motherboard is right at home, as long as she's helping you kill people. She calls herself "Saffak," which almost certainly isn't her real name, but it didn't matter to me either way.

I typed in the license plate and found the car reported stolen, found, and impounded waiting release; a dead end. So I exhaled the scent of the idiots who trashed my apartment into the USB port. Two seconds later I had dossiers on siblings Tim, Gina, and Danny Bianchi—and their sister Mindy, RIP—and a home address for Danny in Olgilvie Moor, one of the newer McMansion clusters off the interstate, a maze of cul de sacs and half-million-dollar homes backed up to state forest. Weird, a family of rats living in a wolf neighborhood. Really weird.

Saffak purred, her fans whirring in that pleased, someone's-gonna-die way she had.

I don't think she cared whether or not that someone was me.

12

Stake-outs are boring as death. Three days of stake-outs in the state forest behind Olgilvie Moor are boring as death and itchy. Between mosquitos and horse flies, I must have lost a pint of blood, but there wasn't any world in which I'd have been dumb enough to storm the place, or even get close enough to trip an alarm—given the number of security cameras dotting the place, there had to be alarms. And wolves weren't the types to call the cops.

Nah. An amateur astronomer's telescope and a wood blind told me everything I needed to know.

One: the Bianchi's were total slobs, denning up in piles of old clothes, half-eaten takeout cartons, cheese-encrusted pizza boxes, and Genny Lite cans, but all the mess was restricted to the inside of the house. The outside remained immaculate, maintained by a truckload of landscapers and gardeners that worked their way through the entire development.

Two: they were on friendly terms with the owner, a wolf named Carl Murray who lived next door. Ex-military, three-piece suit, gold rings and gold chains, he drove a mint Genesis G90 in lime green and wore four thousand dollar shoes. Worked for Lisee Pharmaceuticals, a multinational outfit famous for curing latent vampirism in the early teens. Those bastards cost me a lot of business.

Three: They didn't bother to feed the four girls caged in the basement.

13

I got sick of waiting. These idiots spent all day wallowing in their own filth, smoking blunts and playing video games, and if they cared about Mindy at all it wasn't enough to go to her funeral—closed-casket for what was left of her, municipal lot, no stone.

Murray left his house every day at six a.m. to go for a jog, ran the same route every time tailed by a black SUV loaded with goons, and got home by six forty-five to shower and eat breakfast with his wife—a smokin'-hot brunette whose pre-shower routine involved a couple lines of powder and Cuervo pre-mix chugged from a bottle she kept stashed in the back of their bedroom closet.

I guess margaritas are an anytime food.

Anyway, Mrs. Murray had made a name for herself in the pole-dancing business circa twenty years ago, and by "made a name for herself" I mean "managed not to meth out like everyone else she shared a stage with and retired with all her teeth." Along the way she might have met a dashing young policeman by the name of Mike Szymanski, maybe before his first marriage, before he died the first time.

Back then she went by Starlett Showz, two T's and a Z, but I knew her as Naomi.

14

Fuck it. I rang the bell.

My toe tapped as I waited, and I'd love to say I was keeping the beat with a song in my head, but unless the drummer of that song was a methed-out ferret, I'd have to admit to nerves.

You only get so many true loves, and I'd ploughed through my share.

She opened the door with a sleepy, my-husband-just-left-and-I've-already-chugged-another-quart-of-discount-margaritas-and-done-two-more-lines-of-coke smile. I gave it back, trying to keep the disappointment from my eyes—not at the crow's feet, the thirty extra pounds, the bags under her eyes … everybody gets old. Well, almost everybody. She wanted to be a singer, a dancer, a diva, a star, and here she was, Mrs. Carl Murray, queen of tract housing for rich assholes.

"Hey, Nayo. How's dancin'?"

Her eyes widened, red lips opening in an 'O' of shocked recognition.

"Mikey?"

I pushed past her into the entryway, something I'd done a hundred times under very, very different circumstances, and grunted in surprise at the little .38 revolver she pushed into my gut.

"What are you doing here, Mikey?"

"Me?" I brushed my knuckles across her cheek. "Ain't that the wrong question?"

15

She jammed the gun deeper, cold and hard through my shirt. Her hair smelled like strawberries, her skin like Oil of Olay.

"You still kill people for a living?"

I nodded, once. "A man's got to eat."

"And you're here for Carl."

With a shake of my head, I reached down and put my hand on the gun, closed my warm fingers around hers, cold and papery with years of smoking, drugs, and, well, years. Makeup can hide a lot, but hands always betray you.

"I don't care two shits about Carl. I'm here for the rat problem you got next door."

Her mouth twisted in distaste. "Oh, them."

"Yeah, them. And you know you can't hurt me, so why don't you move this," I said and pushed the pea-shooter down and to the side, stepped into her so that when I looked down our lips almost touched, "and tell me what you know about them."

Her breath mingled the faint brightness of peppermint with fake lime and cheap tequila, but I loved her pouty scowl, and all the other things she could do with that mouth.

"Why don't I just shoot you anyway and feed you to 'em? Could you come back from that?"

I shrugged. "I've had worse."

"Than being eaten by wererats?"

"You bet," I said. "I once had my heart broken by the most beautiful woman in the world."

A hint of a smirk turned up her lips. "Point me at her. I'll kill the bitch."

I kicked the door closed with my heel.

"Nah, Doll, don't do that. Suicide's a sin."

16

Naomi turned on her heel and virtually stalked into the open living room as her flimsy robe fell away, fully exposing the fluorescent green skirt and too-tight red halter that barely contained her curves. She flopped down on the white leather couch and crossed her legs just lazily enough to give a glimpse between—nothing I hadn't seen before, but well worth the look even twenty years later.

Her lazy smile told me she'd caught me, and had been fishing.

"You know Carl will kill you if he finds you here. He doesn't like … competition." The pistol had disappeared during the walk—in a cushion or down her shirt, I had no idea.

Neat trick.

"So he's a legitimate businessman?"

Her slow blink told me nothing. "I thought this was about the neighbors."

I shrugged. "You brought him up."

"Then let's stop talking about him."

"Okay." I sat on the matching loveseat kitty-corner to her, ran my hands across the creamy white leather. "Nice digs. So what's the deal with the rats?"

A tiny quiver shuddered through her, and she tried to hide it with a nonchalant shrug.

"Why do you want to know, Mikey?"

"They tried to kill me."

"Did you deserve it?"

"Probably. But that doesn't mean I'll take it lying down. What's their deal?"

Another shrug. "They keep to themselves."

"Then how about the girls in the basement?"

"What girls?"

"C'mon, Nayo."

"I don't know what you're talking about."

"You can't play stupid. Not with me. I know you way too well."

"It's been twenty years."

"Yeah, but people like us don't change. What am I dealing with, here?"

Her head lolled back on the couch, almost popping her jugs from her top—too bad on the almost—and she groaned, mouth open, eyes wide at the ceiling.

"Why are the men in my life so freaking aggravating?"

I grinned. "Ever tried picking one that ain't a delinquent?"

She snorted.

"Nope."

17

Naomi looked up with a twinkle in her eye, that old familiar smile on her lips.

"What are you doing tonight, Mikey?"

"No," I said. "You're not changing the subject."

"Carl is having a little soirée at La Via. I could get you in."

I shook my head as violently as any head has ever been shookenized.

"Oh, no. I don't mess with leeches. Never have, never will."

She pouted, as fake as it was enticing.

"Oh, come on. I thought you wanted to know about the girls."

I held up my hands as if warding off an unwanted advance—

which, come to think of it, I'd have liked to have been warding off.

"No, no. The rats tried to bump me off. I just want to know why, or who put them up to it. I don't have any track with vampires, and don't want one."

"I never took you for a coward, Mikey."

"I don't have to be a coward to be smart. Nothing good ever came from that mess, and I'm not about to jump in it. The vampire-werewolf thing is way too Kate Beckinsale for my taste, and she only lived through that shit because she was boning the director."

Naomi smiled, bright and happy for the first time. "Do you think she knew?"

"What? That her meal-ticket came from her marital status?" I looked around the douchey McMansion for effect. "How could she not?"

She scowled. "No, dick. That they could get it so wrong."

18

"Yeah," I said. "Who'd have thought that two societies entirely founded on eating people wouldn't be realistic?"

She frowned. "Werewolves don't eat people."

"Well, no more than bankers do."

"Is that a Jewish joke?"

"Nah. Been a long time since I've laid claim to any of that."

"You never struck me as an anti-capitalist."

"Jesus, Nayo. What are you doing, stalling?"

She laughed. "Not anymore."

The door exploded inward, shards of cheap wood peppering us both as a squad of goons burst through the sudden opening. I shot the first between the eyes and dove for cover, but the second opened up with his AK, tearing holes through the loveseat, my clothes, and my torso.

I managed to punch a round through his heart before the third blew my hand to tatters.

Ow.

Carl Murray walked in behind a squad of black-clad goons, each uglier than the last. After he'd been shot.

I sucked air, some of it down my throat, some of it through the holes in my chest.

"The fuck, Carl?" I managed, more wheeze than words.

Carl shook his head, a bemused frown on his face.

"Only you would be stupid enough to come here after I sent people to kill you."

"Why?"

Naomi answered for him. "Why are you so stupid, Babe? Nobody knows."

"But now you're mine," Carl said. "Finally mine."

I dragged my pistol up to my temple, and chuckled through the hurt as the goon squad dove to stop me, stumbling over the Murrays and each other in an effort to reach the gun.

"No!" Naomi cried.

I pulled the trigger.

19

Mom's voice wasn't half as annoying as her old-lady slaps on my cheek, too fast and not hard enough to be anything but an irritation. At least dying hurt, then ended. Her voice carried into the afterlife and beyond, dragging me back to consciousness I didn't deserve and hadn't earned.

"C'mon, Mikey, c'mon. Where's the car, Mikey? Mikey, you there? I told ya not to scratch it. Mikey?"

I groaned, tried to roll away from the mild irritation of her attempts to wake me up and the major irritation of her too-annoying-to-be-Fran-Drescher voice. The slapping stopped; her voice didn't.

Alas.

"I love that car, Mikey. What you do with it?" The slapping resumed. "C'mon, you're almost there. Tell ya mutha, Mikey. Where's the Benz? C'mon Mikey. Wake up, darling boy. Where's my car?"

I smacked her hand away, skin burning at the novel sensation over new nerves.

"Jesus, Ma, stop it!" My throat was so dry you could shake it and serve it to James Bond.

"Now you yell at me, after all I've suffered for you? I bring you back from the dead and this is the thanks I get? Some son you are, lying here all hopeless-like. I should have gotten a puppy. At least it would have loved me. Where's my car?"

I groaned, licked my lips. "I'd have come back anyway, Ma."

"Yeah, but where you'da come back? You think they'd have morgued ya, or dumped you in the swamp again? They're too smart for that, c'mon. Whaddaya doing messing with furries anyway? Ain't nothing but trouble, 'specially now. I raised you smarter, didn't I? Even if you lost my car."

"C'mon, Ma. How long has it been?"

"Almost two weeks. That's what a spleen-grow gets ya."

"Kidney. You only need one, so I can leave the other here. You know that."

I reached down and rubbed the fresh scar on my abdomen—she not only knew that, she'd already taken a new one and put it in the freezer.

"How 'bout smarts, Kiddo, got any of them? Seems my son ain't got none no matter how much brains he's got. You pain me, Son, more than that day I made the mistake of getting a pap smear and a mammogram back-to-back. That was a hell of a day. Where's my fucking car?"

I sighed, long and slow, and imagined lighting her on fire. Just once, just to kill her a while. One glorious minute of her wreathed in golden, flickering flame, followed by a week or three of blissful silence.

Then I returned to reality.

"Jeff's, Ma. It's at Jeff's."

Finally she left the room, swearing about storage fees as she put on her coat. The door slammed as I sat up.

This time I didn't even have underwear on, but hell, it's just family, and I knew where to find some. After all, I'd grown up here.

20

Clothed in fresh jeans and a well-less-than-fresh Rush "Roll the Bones" T-shirt, I took stock of what I thought I knew:

One: the wererats had tried to kill me.

Two: they worked for Carl Murray.

Taken together, that meant they thought they had some way of making it stick, because otherwise why bother?

But …

Three: Naomi knew about the rats, and the girls. And me.

Four: Carl Murray's goons had tried very hard to take me alive.

Which means maybe point one wasn't true.

So if not, what's the game?

I don't blame Naomi for selling out an old flame, especially not to her meal ticket. I just wonder what she thought she knew about me that the wolves would care about. I mean, they couldn't care that I'm an exterminator. The last baron I'd killed was a clean hit, and if I hadn't have taken the job, someone else would have—no way Murray held that against me.

But they sure wanted a piece of me.

I laughed in spite of myself, right there at mom's kitchen table. They had to know they couldn't torture a guy like me, not for anything but fun. So was it fun? Or did he have some other boil on his ass?

And how much did that matter?

The girls. That had to be Naomi. She knew I'd never let innocent kids rot in a basement. Had my number like an old Catholic lady on Bingo night, and I stamped those fucking cards like a Sunday-morning chump.

But just because they were bait didn't mean they weren't in danger.

Shit.

21

If you ever have to sleep on a bench, cover your feet in newspaper. Unless it's the Olympics, nobody pays attention to the homeless, and if you're asleep on a bench with newspaper covering your feet, then you're something less than human, less than worthy of a human's attention.

That sucks. But it's also an opportunity.

The man in the suit passed me without a second glance.

I got up and shuffled after him, and nobody paid me any notice. Five-ten, dudebro haircut, he walked with his head held high, buoyed with self-worth, yet he trucked along with the frantic pace of a man who served impatient masters. But in this kind of crowd, nobody went all that fast, and crazy-eyed when it suited me, even the douchiest of douchebag tourists gave me a wide berth.

Suit-boy walked from Murray's credit union into the Klassy Kitty—a boil on the city's ass but not a place the bouncers would let me through, not in jeans and a T-shirt—and came out three minutes later, sans briefcase. A mule, and too cocky to leave with an identical case.

No surprise. If a cop saw such an obvious move, in this town, they'd be more likely to shake you down for a cut than to turn you in.

Fine, then. The hard way.

It's tough to balance the amount of blunt-force trauma necessary to knock a dude senseless without knocking the senses right out of him, but I counted myself somewhat of an expert on the matter. Suit-boy folded under the sap—a can of dog food wrapped in a sock—and I dragged him into an alley.

22

"Wake up," I said, slapping the kid on the face opposite the soup-can shiner. Jeez, I was turning into my mother.

Kid. Yeah. Early twenties, maybe, just scruffy enough to prove he could grow some scruff, with soft hands and the soft cheeks of someone who'd been hitting the sauce too hard—the spaghetti sauce. He half-kneeled against a dumpster behind the hardware store, ankles hog-tied behind his back to a loop around his neck, arms spread to either side with his wrists tied to the dumpster's feet.

His eyes opened, revealing bloodshot sclera, the left flecked with blood from the can I'd bashed into his temple. Glazed, confused, they widened suddenly and his body flopped against his restraints.

"It's eighth-inch steel wire, kid. You're wasting your time." Five thirty-secondths, but who's counting? "You'll cut your own throat before you break a strand."

"Do you know who I am?"

I kneeled on his left hand, splaying his fingers out against the pavement, and brought the hammer down on his pinky. A wet 'splorch' softened the impact, and blood splattered across my jeans.

As he screamed, I stuffed his jacket sleeve into his mouth—I had his tie and cufflinks in my pocket, both very nice. When he stopped writhing enough so I figure he could understand, I pushed his head back against the cold metal and looked him straight in the frantic, pained eyes.

"Rule number one: I ask the questions. Clear?"

His eyes fluttered, so I hefted the hammer.

"Are we clear?"

He nodded, slow at first and then with some enthusiasm while I tested my grip on the wooden haft, turning the head to catch the metal in the yellow-orange halogen streetlight.

"Rule number two: you get to decide how often I use this. I'd rather not use it again, rather not kill you, either, but figure I've got nineteen tries before I run out of things you can live without. Are we clear?"

Another nod.

"Good. Now I have some questions …."

23

The kid didn't know much.

I sent him home with a bandaged pinky and damaged pride and advice to run, very fast and very far. A risk? Sure. But I'm a big softie. Murray's people would kill him for squealing to me, even if he ratted me out, and maybe he'd stand a chance on the lam … not that wolves enjoyed a hunt or nothing, but despite what they thought, they hadn't been the apex predator hereabouts for a long, long time.

The thing about gangsters you don't really get from TV and movies is just how godawful stupid they are. Their power comes from their brutality, their willingness to inflict pain and suffering and damage beyond what most people could bear, and somewhere in that equation they get cocky and start thinking they're special, that the rules of the universe don't apply to them, that they can buy or fight or kill their way out of anything.

Murray wasn't even alpha wolf, just a high-up enforcer who put the screws to the right bankers and investors to make the pack a whole lot of money—and that made him richer and more successful than most, but still not the king. A king, sure, of pseudo-rich tract housing, complete with his own queen. And some pet rats. And girls in his basement. Girls he'd gotten explicitly to bait me.

According to the kid, those girls had come from the Klassy Kitty, rented by the day against their will from the owner and pimp, a real piece of work named Johnny Honest. Johnny had a few mainstay dancers, but they were just for show. Mostly he liked to trawl schoolyards with his bad-boy good looks, finding young flesh and hooking them on heroin, then hooking them on hooking to pay for the next hit.

He left work most nights at three a.m., with an escort of goons courtesy of his boss to make sure he got home okay. They'd sling him up the highway to his house, let him through the front door, and wish him a good night.

When his keys fumbled in the lock I sat up on the edge of his bed and picked up his shotgun, loaded with silver and pelletized holy water—something told me he didn't quite trust his bosses.

24

It took Johnny ten minutes of dicking around before he made it to the bedroom—putting away dishes, taking out the trash, taking a leak, rubbing one out …. Finally, he walked in, in just his underwear, and flicked on the light. His eyes bugged out when they met the gun barrel.

They were dark brown, and a little too close together. If he was a wolf, he was a mongrel. More likely just a human running with the wrong pack. Either way, the ammo would do the job.

"You know who I am?"

His head shook, but his nervous little eyes didn't believe him, either.

"Try again."

"You gonna shoot me, Szymanski?"

My shoulders twitched, the barest hint of a shrug. "Maybe. Whether or not it's fatally depends on how forthcoming you are."

"Ain't no hits on me right now. Why you even here?"

"This is a pet project. Now spill."

He tried to man-up, but couldn't keep his eyes off the barrel.

"Whaddya wanna know?"

"The girls you sold Murray, he tell you why he needed them?"

"Yep. Bait."

"For me."

He nodded.

"And how long do they have them?"

He shrugged. "Long as they want. They's bought and paid for."

"What happens to them when the wolves are done with them?"

He shrugged and grunted something that might have, in some iteration of the English language, sounded something not utterly unlike "I don't know."

My finger tightened on the trigger.

"Try again."

"They's just girls, man. A million more like 'em every day."

"So the plan is to kill them?"

"Not my plan."

"But the plan."

Another shrug. At least he had the decency to look constipated.

"Why do they want me?"

"I have no fucking idea."

I sighed, long and dramatic. "Look, if I have to say 'try again' one more time, I'm going to blow your brains across that wall."

"They … want what you have."

"And they think they can take it?"

"They do. Got some machine or something to suck it right out of ya."

"That's ridiculous. Ma's a way easier target."

"Too old or something."

I grunted. If that was their problem, they had no idea what they were doing, but if it kept them off Mom's back, it kept them off Mom's back.

"So it's got to be me. And you're in on the take."

"Hell yeah. You'd be, too, if you wasn't you."

"Yeah, living forever's a fucking picnic. You should try it sometime."

"Anyone who ain't you would kill for it. You can't tell me otherwise."

"So you're in. What about the Bianchis?"

He snorted. "Nah, man. The rats don't know shit. Just in it for the crash pad. Think they's living the life."

"Call them. Tell them you got a job for them at Eighth and Barclay."

"What's at Eighth and Barclay?"

"Just make the fucking call."

"And then you'll let me go?"

"Sure."

He made the call, and hung up.

The blast took off most of his skull above his right eye, as you'd think a shotgun at point-blank range would do. I wiped my prints off the gun and dropped it on the floor next to his steaming corpse.

His bowels let go in a flatulent burst as I walked out, perhaps the prettiest thing about his whole damned life.

25

You know what's at the T-intersection of Eighth and Barclay? Not a damned thing. Two vacant lots bulldozed years ago as part of some de-shittification project then left to the weeds, what hardscrabble nonsense could grow amid the cracked asphalt and decaying remains of cinderblocks. Across the street stood a gas station abandoned some time before Eisenhower died, too run down to renovate and too toxic to bulldoze.

A rusty-ass van rolled up across the gas station, tires crackling on gravel. Tim and Danny hopped out, leaving Gina in the driver's seat. Most of these low-level douchebags wouldn't know a woman's value to a job if it bit them on the nuts, and relegated them to getaway driver. Gina was kind of cute for a rat, and Johnny Honest thought with his dick, so maybe she could have helped with the transaction they thought they were about to make. But no, they left her in the van with the keys in the ignition, picking her nails and listening to the radio way too loud.

I knocked on the window with my newest pistol, other finger to my lips.

She looked up, rolled her eyes, and got out of the van as I motioned her to do so.

"Don't say a word," I whispered.

"What—"

Suppressed and subsonic but at two feet away, the bullet entered her left temple at a downward angle, spraying a narrow jot of brains and bits of skull across the side of the vehicle. The idiots leaning against the other side didn't even move as I dragged her out and dumped her behind the rusty pumps, just smoked their cigarettes and talked under the music.

I waited three minutes until their complaints about Johnny's lateness got loud enough to hear over what passed for music, then rounded the corner and double-tapped Danny in the face. As he collapsed, I turned the pistol on Tim, but held my fire.

"Hey, Tim. Sorry 'bout your brother. You want to see your sister again?"

26

Hands at two and ten, Tim Bianchi made the last turn into Murray's cul-de-sac. I looked like shit and smelled worse in his brother's clothes, but with the baseball cap maybe whoever watched the cameras wouldn't notice until far too late. Maybe.

"Where's Gina?" Tim asked.

I rolled my eyes. "She's safe. And if you want her to stay that way you'll shut the fuck up and do what you're told."

"I don't even know what you want."

"And you're not going to." He'd already told me they'd been paid to kidnap me, at least somewhat verifying Johnny Honest's story. "Just pull in the drive and run cover like I told you, and when you get inside I'll get you to your sister."

"You promise she's alive."

"I promise. I'm lots of things, but not a liar. Integrity is everything in this business."

We got out of the van and I kept my head low, followed Tim to the door. He punched in a code and turned the handle as the alarm blipped safe. One hand on his back, I followed him inside and shot him through both lungs in the foyer. He fell on his side, then rolled to his back, mouth opening and closing like a fish.

I fucking hate floppers.

He twitched and spasmed, eyes wide in uncomprehending outrage at my betrayal, chest filling with blood even as is pooled ever-wider across the floor.

I know, I know. I'm a terrible person.

Well, "person."

27

A pair of bolt cutters made short work of the lock on the basement door. I flicked the light and creaked my way down the stairs, nose crinkled against the horrible stench of sickness, piss, and shit. Way too familiar.

"Hey, ladies. You want to get out of here?"

They stared at me with starvation-blackened eyes, young, innocent, uncomprehending. Even after I cut the chain holding them to the radiator, they didn't move, probably fearing some kind of trick.

"There's a van outside. I'm going to take you up there, and we're going to leave." It took two minutes of unbelieved reassurances before I gave up and ordered them upstairs with the gun, barking like a drill sergeant. At the top of the stairs one looked from Tim Bianchi's body to me with the first dawning of hope, and I winked at her.

Her eyes fell, too distrusting of anything remotely human.

We left the cul de sac at seventy miles an hour, but not before I'd doused Murray's house with sixteen gallons of kerosene I'd found in Bianchi's garage, with trails to both propane tanks at the houses to either side. The flames had just started to flicker over the intervening streets by the time we hit the highway. The way reporting goes in this town, I still don't know if the tanks ignited. I'd like to think so. I'd like to think Murray and his goon squad had arrived to see it happen.

"Where are you taking us?" Her voice came out a whisper, cowed and terrified. "Do you have any food?"

I shook my head; born in this kind of starvation, I knew a stop at McDonald's would kill them. "Sorry, toots. You're going to a hospital, and they're going to decide what you eat, and when." A look of alarm crossed her face, so I put my hand on hers, all skin and bones. "I know these people, they're good folks. They'll take good care of you."

"That's what Johnny said," another muttered.

"Yeah, well, Johnny's dead and you're not."

"Really?" All four of them reared back in disbelief.

"Killed him myself, with his own shotgun. Now be quiet."

They didn't say another word except to thank me when the nurses wheeled them away.

Maybe they'd live. Maybe they'd get clean—best I could offer was another chance.

Same as it's always been.

28

I sucked on the cigar and blew a smoke ring out over my bare feet, where it surrounded the sun setting over the rooftops.

"Nasty habit, Johnny," Ma said.

"It's just a cigar."

"Not that, ya putz. I been smoking cigars since Columbus. You think your mother doesn't know a good cigar? You got your feets on the furniture again. You trying to give me pinworms or what? Even an idiot would know better."

"Can we even get pinworms?"

"That's not the point, Mikey. It's just gross."

"Sure, Ma." I put my feet on the floor, thereby increasing my chances of getting pinworms, and downed the rest of my scotch, every bit as hideous as the first time, but it warmed the belly.

We didn't say anything for a while, just waited out the last of the night stars as dawn twilight smothered them in reds and oranges. I stopped breathing until she glared at me, and I heard the unspoken admonishment clear as day—that amateur-hour shit will get you caught.

At last she spoke, but not to yell at me.

"So what about that girl? And the wolf she's with?"

"I don't know, Ma. I think maybe we should skip town. I could become a cop again, you could run another shop, the Szymanskis would fade into memory while we get some ground under us a while. We come back after three or five decades, maybe, and one or both of them'll be dead, and we'll have less to worry about. Everything ties up in a neat little bow. We can keep your house in a dummy holding, pay someone to upkeep it."

"Oh, you think you know what's good for your mother? You think I haven't done enough waiting, Mikey, after Cordoba, after Vilna? Prague? All I ever do is wait, Mikey, wait and wait. Those kids didn't make you for nothing, my darling Son. They made you to save them."

My eyes closed on the encroaching dawn, dark but not dark enough behind heavy lids.

"I know, Ma, I know. It's been eighty years, and all I can taste is paper. And those kids, they got to be dead by now." I took another pull off the cigar. "All of 'em. Who's left to save?"

"There's always more kids, Mikey. And that broad of yours, she's up to no good."

Another puff, another dark thought, and I almost put my feet up just to spite her.

I hated when she was right, but she was right, and there wasn't no running from it. Born with a mission in my mouth, I couldn't walk away from it no matter what I believed, no matter what it cost me, no matter if those who gave it to me lived on through their children's children but rested in the ground themselves.

And yeah, I didn't know what craziness Murray and his pack dreamed they had on me, and had no idea what I'd do about Naomi, but I literally don't have it in me to run away.

So when the clock hit eight I called up Tony Wheels for a new van, still on the house for saving his great-grandfather from the camps. The sixth van he'd given me, and every one a gift I didn't deserve. Still, it paid to have friends.

The extermination business ain't glamorous, but it keeps the lights on.

A TASTE FOR LIFE

"And how old were you when you died, Mister Beauchamp?" Joan Rothman asked, leaning back in her chair. The scientists watched her behind the one-way mirror, hands clasped behind their backs.

"Twenty-seven," the corpse replied, more gurgle than speech, as it gazed idly around the interview room.

Joan jotted down the response, then chewed pensively on the tip of her red pen. The lights flickered as the air circulators shuddered to life in the depths of the bunker, filling the observation room with a faint scent of bleach and formaldehyde.

She crossed her legs and rested the clipboard between her knee and the folding table, unknowingly flashing her slip to the men behind the mirror.

Bhim Raychaudhuri smiled appreciatively at the view and spoke into the microphone wired to her ear bead. "Math, Miss Rothman."

"Thank you," she said to the creature, making no sign that she'd heard the command. "And how old are you now?" She poised the pen above the clipboard.

The corpse scowled, the pallid flesh of its forehead wrinkling in concentration under the single naked bulb. "What year is it?"

"It's twenty sixty-seven, Mister Beauchamp."

"What month?" it asked.

"April, Mr. Beauchamp. On the surface it's springtime."

"And I died in two thousand twelve?" it asked, wheezing.

"As near as we can tell, Mister Beauchamp."

It grunted, a flatulent gasp of rotten breath, and scowled down at its manacled hands. It shifted its weight in the folding chair, and its good eye lolled up to look at her face.

"I'm hungry."

She nodded. "Food is coming. Please be patient, Mr. Beauchamp."

"Real food?" the corpse asked, leaning forward in anticipation.

Joan didn't answer. Her eyes flicked toward the mirror.

Behind the glass, Bhim took off his spectacles and polished them as he turned to his partner. "Well, it looks like the memory recovery works."

Mike Reed nodded reluctantly. "Yeah, I suppose, if you remind it who it is all the time. But they still can't do simple arithmetic." He stretched one crooked finger toward the mirror. "Look at it, our most promising subject, fidgeting and hiding behind the hunger to avoid answering the question. That's pretty disappointing."

"Baby steps, Mike. Last time he couldn't even remember his name."

Mike shoved his finger under Bhim's nose. "Don't you 'baby step' me, Bhim. The time before it remembered its name *and* calculated its age! Is two-digit subtraction too much to ask?"

Bhim chuckled. "No, but that time he also tried to feed on Joan after three minutes of questioning. Look!" He pointed at the analog clock hanging on the wall. "It's been nearly twenty minutes, and he's only now beginning to show the signs. The serum works."

They turned their attention back to the room, where Joan kept nervously glancing in their direction. The men sighed in unison.

"Okay," Mike said. "Feed it and get it back to its cage. We'll try Mister Lamandola."

Four months later, Mister Beauchamp sat at the same table, staring uninterestedly at the voluptuous form of Joan Rothman. Bhim's grin was infectious, but Mike possessed strong antibodies to good humor.

Mike grabbed the microphone and barked, "Tell it to stop stalling and tell us!"

Joan cringed at the volume, then composed herself. She reached across the table and supportively squeezed the dead thing's hand. "Please, Mister Beauchamp. It's been nine weeks since you've fed. How often do you think about it?"

It lifted its dead eye and regarded her flatly. It licked its lips, an all-too-human gesture with no biological purpose.

"All the time, Miss Rothman. All the time. It's hard to think about anything else."

Behind the mirror, Mike grunted. "You see? It's like a child molester. All we've done is suppress it."

"Hush," Bhim said.

"Really?" Joan asked. "Even now, when I was reading to you? After all this time we've spent together?"

Beauchamp's lips peeled back, revealing black, rotten teeth; a smile. "It consumes me."

"But you control it," she said, slowly retracting her hand. "Why?"

"It makes me human," he replied. "Your serum. It makes the urge … Not less, but somehow controllable. I don't need it anymore. I just want it."

Bhim didn't need to look at Mike to feel the 'I told you so' eyes boring into his skull.

"What about the food we give you, Mister Beauchamp? Meat? Bread? Water?" Joan asked.

"Call me Jason." It wasn't a request.

"Ok, Jason, what about the food we give you? Doesn't it satisfy you?"

Jason shook his head. A clump of hair tumbled to the floor.

"Increased physical degeneration," Mike said.

"Shut up!" Bhim replied. "I'm trying to listen."

"… like it. Do you like steak?" it asked.

Joan nodded.

The zombie gurgled. "I used to love steak. All food, really. I was a chef …" It stared at her longingly.

Joan tapped the intercom twice. She was getting nervous.

"But now?" she asked. Outwardly, she was cool as ice.

"Now it all tastes like nothing." It continued to leer at her with its good eye, its bad eye drifting lazily around the room. "I move, but I don't live. I don't taste anything. I can't feel anything. But that's not the worst of it …"

She tapped the intercom again. "What's the worst of it, Jason?"

"Shouldn't we—" Mike started.

"*Shush!*" Bhim's eyes didn't twitch from the scene in front of him.

It hesitated. "The worst of it …" It froze.

Joan waited.

"The worst is that I don't want anything. Anything at all."

The intercom clicked again, twice. "So the serum works, Jason?" she asked. "You said you don't need to feed now."

"I don't *need* to. Haven't for weeks. I'm not mindless, you know."

She smiled at him.

Here it is, Bhim thought.

"What would you do if we set you free, Jason?"

"That's simple," it said. "I'd kill you all. And then I'd eat your brains."

Mike screamed in frustration.

Bhim chuckled despondently. "We're never getting out of this bunker, are we?"

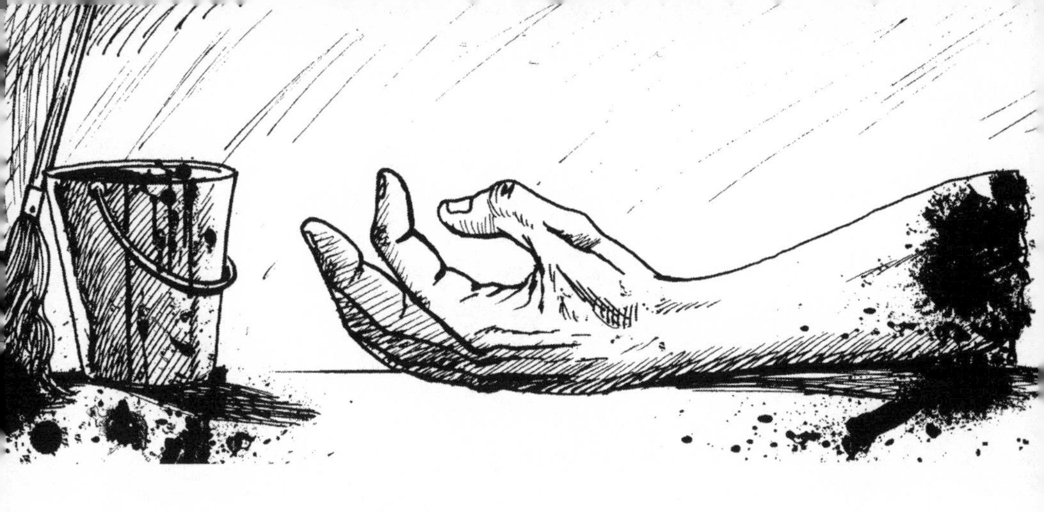

TWELVE KILOS

Bright red blood squirted between blazing orange polyfiber strips, and Darren's stomach growled. He twisted the mop again and cursed every droplet that escaped the bucket, destined for the rusted metal grate in the floor. Two, maybe three milliliters spilled per job. Sixteen jobs a day, seven days a week didn't add up to much, but it did add up. A liter a month might move his family to a higher level, farther from the heat of the core. But this month he wouldn't even keep his family from the tithe, and he had no one to blame but himself.

Jacelyn heaved the last body onto the autoloader and wiped her red-stained hands on its shirt. He hid his envy. Damned meaters never had to worry about spillage. Meat wouldn't flop down the drain, wouldn't soak into clothes and mops and hair. One, maybe two meaters a month didn't buy out their tithe. A life of luxury.

The body flopped over onto its back, and Darren sighed as he recognized its face. Hal couldn't have been more than sixteen, and he and Darren's daughter Felicity had been friends of a sort. A kid that sloppy never should have been a harvester in the first place; lost a kidney last week, a good six feet of intestines the month before, and that's no way to buy out. A matter of time, this.

His stomach rumbled again.

Jacelyn's smile distracted him from his reverie, rotted teeth behind pale lips in a face that might once have been pretty. It held more pity than scorn, and he didn't need a meater's sympathies, no matter how well intentioned. Sure, blooding came hard, harder still to those with mouths to feed, but an honest day's work took effort, and let it never be said he didn't try his best. To break her gaze he pulled his lunch from his pocket, tore open the pouch, and squeezed the gelatinous contents into his mouth. The vegetal, hydroponic slime drowned out the iron tang of blood-stench for two gulps.

His muscles strained as he lifted the bucket onto the hover lift, and he held his breath in anticipation as he swiped his finger across the bar code. He knew, but he didn't want to.

"Thirty-nine point four kilograms," the mechanical voice read, dispassionate in its pronouncement. The lift disappeared into the ceiling and he turned around, shoulders slumped. The priest emerged from the wall, a tangle of wires and tubes in a parody of humanoid form, three yellow glass eyes glowing too bright from clusters of internal LEDs.

He bowed his head in fear and shame, and shivered as the cold metal fingers ran through his hair. It took his mother's voice, as it always did, but none of her tone. "Blooder Darren, your monthly tithe is fourteen thousand four hundred kilograms. The counters tally fourteen thousand three hundred eighty-eight kilograms. Do you acknowledge the discrepancy?"

He licked his chapped lips. "There weren't enough bodies brought—"

"Do you acknowledge the discrepancy?"

"I do," he blurted.

"And you accept the responsibility of failure?"

"I do."

"Then pray."

They said it together, his exhausted rasp mingling with his long-dead mother's dulcet monotone. "May the World-Machine forgive my inadequacies. As we sacrifice, so does It, that in Its eternal hunger and torment it might keep us from the Pit Eternal. Amen."

The priest continued. "In reflection of Its pain, return to your home and prepare."

He kept his eyes closed as the priest withdrew. He opened them to Jacelyn's, bright and blue and centimeters from his face. She kneeled in front of him, work suit soaked with sweat.

"How bad?" Her warm breath reeked of onion and rot.

"Twelve kilograms."

She hissed in a breath. "The tithe, then?" It wasn't a question, and he didn't respond. After a moment she stood, and the bloody smears on her knees mocked him. "Maybe they'll—"

"Just don't." He took her offered hand and let her drag him to his feet. "I've missed quota three times in five years, but never by more than five. Twelve? They won't forgive that."

"They might. You're a good worker, one of the best blooders I've ever seen. They have to see that—"

"No, they don't. The World-Machine knows no compassion or love or virtue or vice—"

"—only hunger and sacrifice, that it might keep us from the Pit Eternal," she finished. "Amen." Her hand on his shoulder left a red-brown streak. "You're right. I'm sorry."

He left her there, frowning after him, as he punched out and showered before the trip home. Hot water cascaded down his face when the claxon sounded the arrival of another trainload. He'd toweled off before the gunfire began, and wondered which lucky blooder had taken his place.

Ona's heart broke when she met him at the door, eighty minutes early from a ten-hour shift. She didn't say anything, but he saw it as he brushed black ringlets from her pale face, wrinkled and tight but still beautiful even with tears she couldn't afford to shed filling her eyes. And then she said nothing, and neither did he, even when Felicity broke down in tears and ran to hide in her room.

He kissed his wife, first her cheek, and then the stub of each hand as she brought them to his lips, the daily gesture a reminder of his unbroken promise those many years ago. *As the World-Machine protects us, I will protect you, to the end of all days, to the edges of the Pit, forever and always.*

A lesser man would have abandoned her after the accident sixteen years prior. A man of his talents could have had anything; an apartment near the surface where the air came fresh through the purifiers, where shimmers of sunlight might reflect down the shafts to warm his face. He did the work of three, and could have anything that would pay for.

But he wanted only her, and their daughter, and that meant buying out three tithes. Three tithes at thirty kilograms a day, seven days a week. Fourteen thousand four hundred kilograms a month, fourteen thousand forty-eight liters of blood—depending on iron content. His mother told him he couldn't do it, right up until the moment she stumbled naked and crying from the train car. His father told him he couldn't do it, but loved him for trying.

But he did it. For sixteen years he'd bought out three tithes, twice or more what any other blooder could manage. He'd killed seven men and four women in fights for the largest puddles, and even with the forfeiture of their blood he earned the right to live, the right for his family to live. His daughter, the spitting image of her mother decades past, his loving wife, and himself. Now one of them had to die.

He never should have picked up that bucket. Flush with morning's energy, he'd filled it too full, and in his haste he'd slipped. It hit the ground in a geyser, showering him, showering Amy, who laughed and licked it from her lips. She never saw the energy beam that vaporized half her head for her blasphemy, and they'd docked Darren's tithe as if he'd killed her, five-point-three kilograms on top of the fourteen he'd spilled. His appeal had fallen on deaf ears, and though he'd worked as hard as he could those last few hours, he just couldn't make up the difference.

"My love?"

He shook off his thoughts and tried to smile. Ona hugged him, and whispered in his ear.

"We knew this day would come. You've given me so much time, so much I wouldn't have had. It's time to let go."

He shook his head. *No, no, no, never.*

Behind him Felicity echoed his defiance, amplified it. "No. We can run. We don't have to do this."

They turned together, mouths open in shock.

"Honey," Darren said, "you can't defy the World-Machine. It protects us from—"

"No. It doesn't protect anybody. It feeds on us, uses us. It's nothing but a—"

He slapped her, and slapped her again when she opened her mouth to continue. "Where did you hear these blasphemies?"

She shook her head. "No, I won't say."

"But you'll repeat them." Ona's soft rebuke did what his slaps could not.

Felicity's eyes blazed, but she cast them downward. "I will repeat them. And repeat them and repeat them, until you understand. There is no Pit, or if there is we live in it. The resistance—"

Darren grabbed her shoulders. "The World-Machine is all that stands between us and the Pit. It can't survive without us, so we do as we must to feed it. If we fail, all is lost. The resistance is work of the Enemy."

A hint of a sneer crept to her lips. "You feed the Enemy."

He stepped back. "What?"

"The surface is clean, pure. Anyone can live there."

Ona shook her head. "Sweet daughter, they've fed you lies."

"I've been there."

His hand stung as he backhanded her to the floor, and he cried out as he kicked her. "You will not blaspheme in my presence, daughter."

Huddled on the floor, arms wrapped around her legs, she whimpered. "I've been there, and it's beautiful."

He reared back, and Ona stopped him with a touch. He closed his eyes and fought to compose himself, and dropped to his knees.

His wife spoke for him, knowing his mind better than he did. "Explain yourself, daughter."

"Liam resists. I've traveled with them, beyond the high levels to the surface itself. The sun doesn't burn your flesh, there is no radiation. Animals cavort in gentle sunlight, plants—green plants!—flourish under blue skies. And rain! You wouldn't believe rain, even if I showed it to you. Fresh water falls from the sky to nourish the land below. You wouldn't believe."

Darren opened his mouth, but Ona cut him off. "You swear this? On your life you swear this?"

"I do."

"Then tell us how to get there." He and Ona locked eyes over their daughter.

But Felicity shook her head. "You'll betray us. I know you, father, and I know you, mother, and I know you're too loyal, and that you have to see it first to believe. We live in the Pit, and your lives are dedicated to keeping us there."

"Daughter," Darren said. "I warned you."

Ona kissed his cheek, and he fell to her calming warmth. "Let me talk to her," she whispered.

The girls went into the bedroom, the only other room in their tiny apartment, and while they talked Darren slept as an acolyte should. Energy controlled everything they did, every shred they used for themselves a selfish denial of the World-Machine, every Joule a sacrilege to the agony It suffered on their behalf. He woke when footsteps intruded on his dream.

Ona bowed her head, eyes cast to the floor. "She's sleeping."

"As is right," they intoned together.

He brushed her cheek with his fingertips, an electric thrill even after all these years. They'd chosen.

They cried together, and made frantic, desperate love on the floor, and cried again and again. And then he opened a channel. His mother's voice answered.

He jostled awake, and brushed his daughter's hand from his shoulder. "What time is it?"

"An hour before morning claxon. Let's go."

He stumbled to his feet, still in his travel clothes from the day before. He stepped toward the bathroom and his daughter shoved him toward the front door. "There's no time! Just go."

He paused. The turn of a knob, and his daughter would feed

the World-Machine. A step into darkness, and his family would die. Would Ona's love die with their daughter? Would his?

He turned the handle and stepped outside, running his tongue over gritty teeth. The lights would come on only at claxon, so darkness consumed everything. "Fel, we're—" he breathed a sigh of relief as three yellow eyes blinded him from everything else. "Come, daughter. It's time to go."

Agony wracked him, more than he thought possible. *Despair is a sin*, he thought, but the thought didn't save him. It took an eternity to realize the pain wasn't emotional, wasn't spiritual. Three yellow eyes dimmed, disappeared, became two. Green, not yellow. Liam's. His daughter's voice accompanied him to the afterlife.

"It's okay, dad. It's okay."

He woke to an alien world. Blue blazed above him, an unrelenting brightness that penetrated to the core of his being. He turned from it, tried to see in the unrelenting light, could just make out humanoid shapes in a sea of soft green. *The priests have come.*

A step forward, then two. Something tickled his feet, a scattering of tiny strips like his mop, green instead of orange. Delicate, they crushed underfoot. He breathed deep, and couldn't describe the joy contained in that air. Life, hope, happiness, he'd never known an aroma so rich.

A silhouette filled his vision, black curls and pale skin, delicate hands in a blue dress.

"Hi, papa. Welcome to the surface."

He reached out, grabbed her, pulled her to him. "What is this?"

"This is truth. Our life underground, that's the lie."

"No." He shook his head and buried it in his daughter's shoulder. "My whole life, the things I've done. It needs me. It needs us."

"No, dad. It used you. It used me and your mother and everyone you've ever known. The World-Machine is the Pit."

He cupped her cheeks, then dropped his hands to her neck. Her pulse quickened under his callouses, a desperate flutter unhinged from reason. He squeezed. "Liar." She clawed at him, raked her nails across his hands, drew precious microliters of blood but didn't, couldn't, diminish his purpose. "You want me to give up my wife. You want me to live a blasphemy. I cannot. I will not. I. Will. Not."

"Darren!"

He turned at his wife's shriek, almost let go of their daughter. Her struggles weakened, and he squeezed harder.

Something large and pale filled his vision, then his head exploded in pain.

On his knees, he struggled to regain his feet. Another explosion of light and pain, and he lay on the green strips. *Grass. This is grass.* His mind plucked the fact from somewhere, childhood movies from before the Scouring or fairy tales from his father.

"Yes, father," Felicity said, and he realized he'd spoken aloud.

He looked up, and found his daughter holding hands with their neighbor, the sandy-haired boy Liam.

They smiled at him, sad and hopeful.

"It's impossible. But it's real. Everything you've known is a lie. When we go back—"

Darren shook his head. "No. We can't go back. I've betrayed you. You and Liam. They're going to take you for the tithe. If we go back, you'll die."

Liam's smile held no warmth. "We know. And it's too late to do anything about that. But you can do something. You can bring it down. Save humanity from the Pit."

"No, it doesn't have to be like this. I can—" A sharp pain stabbed into his neck, and the world swam, then went dark.

Darren shook the cobwebs from his head. A cacophony filled his ears—gunfire and screaming and laughter—and then only laughter. He rushed forward, mop in hand, bucket handle tucked into his elbow, as he'd done a thousand times.

The first body lay face-down, a sandy-haired man, too lean, too young. Another lay next to him, her mangled, naked body twisted into a parody of human form, but still she held his hand. Jacelyn tore them from one another, and he refused to see their faces. He shoulder-blocked Curt out of the way with a feral snarl, smeared the polyfiber strips through the wet, red liquid, and squeezed it into the bucket.

The priests had given him another chance. They'd given him new life, new purpose. Three hundred sixty-five days, fourteen thousand four hundred kilograms.

And yet ....

FOAM RIDE

"Do you want the fucking job or not?" Barry slammed down his Mai Tai, the orange-red liquid sloshing over the glass onto his hand, his intense glare boring holes through Alyssa's skull.

She brushed sand off her leg as an excuse to control her actions. "Of course I do." Punching him here wouldn't do any good anyway, and he brought her quality work by the bucket. Like this job for twenty-five thousand euros, almost six month's rent, four after catching up on what she owed.

"Then what's the problem?"

She looked out across the water, a crystal blue too pure for nature. The sand squished between her toes well enough, but she could just make out the thin haze of pixel blur around the horizon, Barry's telltale architecture glitch. "You said 2008. So what's the scam? Who's the client you're ripping off?"

He sucked sticky liquid from his fingers, obviously stalling. "Not until you sign."

She leaned forward with a scowl. "I'm not in the fraud business."

"It's not fraud."

"'Course it is. There aren't any pads in '08." She twirled a finger around a lock of dark brown hair, enjoying the sensation while she had it. It helped her control her temper; maybe growing it out again wouldn't be a bad idea. She ran a hand over her scalp—her real scalp, back in her living room—and suppressed a sigh at the prickly stubble around the neural jacks. Her avatar maintained a look of bored, somewhat hostile disbelief.

"He insists there is. A first-gen prototype."

She froze.

Barry laughed, a hearty bellow too loud over the artificial surf. "Why do you think you're getting paid so much?"

In her room she reached for her head jack. The smell of diaper and litter box and poverty crept in as she let her consciousness drift to the real world, and she stayed her hand. "I want a million euros."

Barry raised an eyebrow. "For a foam ride?"

She snapped her fingers, and above her hand a hologram appeared. The most famous monkey in the history of history, Koko had been the first primate to travel through time and survive. His mangled, pulsing muscles shivered, exposed to the air in thousands of places. Tufts of fur smoldered where he had skin at all. "I got kids to feed, so if I'm risking that kind of ride, a million euros or fuck off."

"The control comes from now, not then. You won't have issues just because the landing pad's a prototype. Eighth-generation quantum foam software, sixth generation hardware, everything state-of-the-art."

"A million, or find somebody else."

"Done."

Barry said it so fast she didn't have time to react.

A million euros.

"W—what's the job, then?"

A stack of papers appeared on the table in front of her, held down at the corner by her Corona. She flipped through them. "Wait, this job is for Seth Newell?"

"Yeah, why?"

Memories savaged her; sleepless nights spent talking despite finals week, shared experiences of orphanages and foster care, sweat and heartbeats and shared breath in the back of an ancient Camaro, a white dress and an altar and vows unsaid.

She schooled her face to flat neutrality. "Why would Seth want to bring down the company he helped found?"

"Newell never forgave Dean Crossing for taking Foam Tech public, didn't think the public was ready, or responsible enough, for time travel."

She snorted. "He was right. What have we done with it besides screw people?"

Barry shrugged. "You can't change the past—"

"—just snoop around in it," she finished for him. "How many people have you blackmailed with the information I've given you? How many companies—lives—have you destroyed?"

He shrugged, a massive heave of massive shoulders. "You take the jobs."

"Yeah, but I don't like it. What's he going to do with the information? Pandora's Box had the lid blown off." She read further, enlarging the text for her tired eyes. "That's it? A million cash to get the number off a rabies tag?"

"That's it."

She dropped the papers and locked eyes with him. "What's the catch?"

"The catch is that that dog tag holds the final decryption code for Foam Tech's mainframe, and if they find out you're after it they'll kill you and everyone you know. And you'll be going to a prototype pad. *The* prototype pad."

"I thought you said it was safe."

"We're pretty sure it is. They're almost to the point where a landing pad is outmoded tech."

"That's impossible."

He shrugged again. "Was impossible. Soon it won't be."

"So why not wait and do the job once it's possible?"

"Client wants it done now. He can't get any younger."

She weighed the risks and wondered how much she trusted Barry. "Alright. Wire the money."

She yanked out the jack and shuddered as reality slammed in. Dropping the metal probe into the bleach solution, she whirled around in her chair and smiled at Tyler, still on the floor pushing around a toy maglev train. "You," she booped his nose, "need a diaper change."

He reached up as she inserted sterile plastic plugs into the holes in her cranium. That done, she lifted him, grunting at the weight, and carried him through the tiny kitchen into the nursery. A plastic crib, faded and cracked, lurked in the corner next to a dim lamp.

What kind of crib can a million euros buy?

Alyssa tossed a meager tip at the cabbie and got out, feeling under-dressed in her most expensive dress, a blue faux-silk, with synthetic sapphire earrings to match. A brown wig covered her bald head, freshly shaved in preparation for the night's job. Cars passed, sleek Motoyamas and TetraTeslas, with the occasional vintage gasoline retrofit BMW or Mercedes-Benz, rumbling with artificial engine noise. She shuffled, uneasy and out of place, toward Seth Newell's mansion. No, scratch that. Palace.

The sprawling campus held four buildings, squat edifices of peach brick and stark white mortar behind a black iron fence twenty feet high. She identified herself at the intercom and they buzzed her through. Slate pavers meandered through lush gardens of flowers and citrus trees and green grass, a fortune spent on fresh water in a world running dry. Servos whined as cameras tracked her progress up the walk, rendering the lighted doorbell almost quaint. She rang it anyway, with a single lacquered nail, for half a second.

Seth opened the door himself. She wasn't sure why that surprised her, but it did. She took in his boyish grin and sandy, sloppy hair and easy stance, vestiges of the boy she knew from a lifetime ago. The crow's feet were new, and the thousand-euro shirt. She smirked at his bare feet before meeting his gaze. They held what her mother had called "the W's": wary, weary, wise. It took a special kind of person to lie with their eyes, and no amount of coaching on her part had made him any better at it.

"Al!" He hugged her, lean muscle and subtle aftershave, and mumbled into her ear. "It's been too long." He steered her through a foyer bigger than her apartment, her heels clacking on stone tile.

"Granite floors?"

He chuckled, a tinge of red gracing his cheekbones. "Grandiose, I know. When you run in my circles, you have to have what other people don't, or they won't respect you. You should see the elevators."

"You have elevators in a three-story building?"

"Most of the complex is underground."

They entered an intimate kitchen, almost too clean, with stainless steel appliances and a small island for eating. He pulled open the fridge, grabbed a beer, and with a grin handed her a diet Dr. Pepper.

"No way!" She twisted off the cap and swilled the delicious, ice-cold beverage.

"You drank the same thing for four years straight."

"… and you just happened to have some on hand, in case I stopped by after fifteen years?"

His grin vanished. "You talked to Barry. I knew you'd be by."

She froze mid-swig, lowered the bottle. "I did. And here I am."

"Your price go up?"

She laughed, a humorless, quiet thing dead on arrival. "Had I known it was you, I'd have asked for ten million."

He said nothing for a moment. "Did I really hurt you that much?"

She set down the drink and hugged him, and her lips brushed his ear. "Yeah, but it was a long time ago, and I forgave you the moment it happened." She pulled back, patted his cheek, and stared into his baby blues. "You weren't ready and I pressured you and you loved her, too, and that's okay. We're adults. We thought we were adults then and know better now."

He sighed, and she continued.

"But that's not why. I'd ask for ten million because you've got more money than God."

His cheeks reddened further and he looked at the floor. "If you needed help, you only had to ask."

"I don't need your help." She barked a bitter laugh at their respective career paths, his meteoric, hers through the mud. "I need a paycheck, and you're asking me to do something insanely dangerous. A ride into a prototype pad could turn me into scrambled eggs."

"Then don't do it."

She raised an eyebrow. "You're the one hiring me."

"I could hire someone else."

"Do you want to?"

"No."

She stared into those triple-W baby blues and watched his pupils flash, his lids tense just a hair. *Why are you lying to me, Seth?* She licked her lips, formulated a dozen replies, and said none of them.

He broke eye contact to look out the quaint window above the quaint sink, at the majestic and not-at-all quaint garden exploding with color only the fabulously wealthy could hope to own.

He cleared his throat. "This could be dangerous."

"Yup."

"Not just the foam ride. If they catch wind and send someone back—"

"I've dealt with rivals in the past." She snorted. "Literally."

"Don't underestimate these people. I trust you to do this, but don't want you getting hurt."

She shrugged. "We know I don't die."

He shook his head. "C'mon, you know better. Just because nobody's ever found your body doesn't mean you didn't die. Totally different things."

She smirked. "Do you think I'm going to die?"

"No." His eyes told the same truth as his mouth.

"Are you certain?"

"Nobody can be certain."

Another lie.

"A million euros, then."

"Yes."

Why does this make you so sad, babe?

She stepped into the launch pad, a cylinder of brushed chrome as featureless on the inside as out. In a vintage T-shirt, blue jeans, and sandals, she looked the part of an early-century woman, save for the cranial jacks, which she covered with a bleach-blonde wig. Her backpack, also vintage, held only the essentials: a ski mask, brass knuckles, a B&E kit, and two kilograms of beef jerky.

"In position?" Barry asked through the intercom. She didn't know where he really was, and it didn't matter. Nobody could match his ability at manipulating quantum foam to stimulate temporal slide.

"In position."

"Looks like your ride's for nineteen minutes, plus or minus. Dean built the pad in a storage shed in the back yard, and every story he's ever told indicates he couldn't get it to work and abandoned it there until he finished his first bachelor's degree … in ninth grade. So you shouldn't have any spectators. Get in, read the tag, and hide until you ride back. Good to go?"

"Do it."

Tiny beams of sunlight illuminated motes of dust kicked up by her arrival. She coughed into the crook of her elbow and waited for her eyes to adjust. The landing pad didn't look like a prototype, it looked like a junk pile. Wires and tubes snaked everywhere over a stainless steel grid, a twisted mélange of spaghetti wiring. She never would have agreed to the jump had she seen the landing pad first. Still, nobody could beat Barry at his job, and the foam ride had been both painless and instantaneous.

The storage shed—more of a rickety wooden shack—held massive piles of old tech: laptop computers, photomultiplier tubes, smart phones, oscilloscopes, and heaps of engineering-related equipment she didn't recognize. Amidst the tech stood rakes, shovels, a stack of faux-clay pots, and several bags of red cedar mulch. A paper wasp nest buzzed in the far corner; the insects paid her no attention whatsoever.

A peek out the door crack yielded the expected intel, a fenced-in yard with a dog pen and two young maple trees behind a double-wide trailer with cracked, peeling siding that might once have been a light beige. Contrasting this humble beginning with Dean Crossing's multitrillionaire lifestyle made her brain hurt. She opened the door with a lazy creak, stepped out, and approached the trailer. En route she put on the mask, but kept it bunched on her head like a cap.

A peek inside the back window told her everything she needed to know: a female pit bull with a black and brown brindle coat snoozed on her back, legs spread, in the middle of the single unmade bed in the back of the living area. The pink collar looked promising. Laundry covered every surface—the bed, both chairs, the tiny kitchen table. Lace panties hung even from the kitchen faucet, but at least they looked clean. Aside from the dog and a dubious plate of what might have been food some months ago next to the preposterously thick 2DTV, there were no signs of life.

She crept around to the front of the house and put her hand on the front door handle. The cheap aluminum blazed in the afternoon sun, almost too hot to touch. She opened the outer door, tried the inner knob. Locked, of course. She knelt, pulled out the B&E kit, set the brass knuckles on the ground, and opened the bag of jerky. If Fido wasn't friendly, she might be more interested in food than guard duty.

She jammed the shim through the door and lifted, wiggling until it jammed in next to the deadbolt. She twisted, released, twisted again. Eighty seconds later she opened the door and stepped inside with her gear, a smile on her face and bag of jerky in-hand.

The dog bounded to her, tail wagging, eyes bright and happy.

"Hi, puppy!" She upended the bag on the kitchen floor, and the dog went to town, gobbling down morsels without bothering to chew. She grabbed the collar and looked at the tag. BERNIE. "Are you a good girl, Bernie?" Bernie ignored her in favor of jerky, tail beating against her legs. She turned the collar—harder than it should have been, but the nylon squeezed too tight and Bernie's neck rippled with hard muscle.

Another twist revealed the number: 254-469-2848-74. She reached under her wig and pressed the cylinder in her memory jack, saving the data. "Good girl!" She patted the dog on the head.

"Excuse me," a woman said behind her.

She whirled to find a blonde girl, no more than twenty-five, in a Pearl Jam T-shirt and Daisy Dukes, fists on her hips, stance wide just inside the door. Pretty in a way, her skin pulled too tight on her face, her eyes still baggy and dark under too much makeup. She sneered at

Alyssa with teeth brown from methamphetamine abuse.

"What the hell do you think you're doing?"

"Sorry, I was—"

The woman kicked, a practiced move more Tai Bo than Tai Kwon Do. Alyssa dropped prone, then leapt to her feet, brass knuckles in hand. "I don't want to hurt you."

"Fuck you, bitch." She drew out the last word to two syllables, "bee-itch," as she pulled a steak knife from the counter. And then she swung. Alyssa blocked the swing and drove brass knuckles into her assailant's solar plexus. She dropped to the ground without even catching herself, a dull thud and a clatter of steel on linoleum.

The woman coughed, and blood sprayed from her mouth. Her eyes open, she didn't blink, and after a haggard breath didn't move, or twitch. Alyssa sighed, a sad acknowledgement of the loss of life.

You can't change the past.

She'd killed this woman twenty-five years ago.

"Dammit, lady, there's no way I hit you that hard."

Bernie, done with her snack, licked the dead woman's face and whined, smearing red blood across her haggard features.

Her internal clock gave four minutes to ride. Give or take. She turned to leave and a school bus stopped right in front of the driveway. A young boy, maybe ten or eleven, bounded down the stairs, laughing at something. His light brown, almost sandy hair and boyish smile drove a knife into her heart, his baby blues killing her as surely as she'd killed his mother.

This isn't Dean Crossing's house.

He got the mail and ran toward the door. Bernie bolted outside, tail wagging, the stupid dog unable to process what she'd witnessed through the joy of her boy coming home. She ran in joyous circles around the boy, lunging and running away and lunging again, and oh how he laughed.

She stepped into the darkness, pulling the mask over her face.

"Mom?" Seth cried out.

She bolted into the bedroom and tried to lock the door, but it had no lock. She closed her eyes and fought back tears.

"Mom? Mom!" His cry went from worried to heart-wrenching

anguish. She stumbled back, unwilling to hear any more but unable to escape, and a lamp crashed down behind her.

"Who's there?" Footsteps, then a fist pounding on the door. "I'll *kill* you, you motherfucker! If it's the last thing I do. I'll fucking—"

She closed her eyes against the bright white glare off the stainless steel tube. She let out a breath she didn't know she'd been holding, choked down the nausea always felt on return to the present.

"Welcome back," Barry said. "Sixty-seven microsecond slide, a hundred forty-eight petajoules net loss." His perfunctory tone softened. "You look like shit."

The cylinder lifted with a whine of servos. Seth Newell sat against the wall, hands in his lap. Wet streaks marred his cheeks. "She should."

She held up her hands, and realized the brass knuckles still constricted her fingers.

"Is that how you did it? Is that how you killed my mother?"

"Hey now," Barry's voice rang out. "Everything up-and-up there?" Seth touched a button on the wall, killing the intercom.

"I hit her once, just to knock her down," she said. "It shouldn't have killed her." Lame, as apologies went.

"Years of methamphetamine abuse, coupled with syphilis and a couple of other things. She was a junkie hooker, but she was my mom. And you hit her hard enough to burst her pancreas."

"I'm so sorry."

"It took me a while to figure out what happened, that someone used the prototype to come back for something. I've spent my whole life figuring out who. Do you know how many people I've sent back? How much money I've spent, how many years, to find the person who killed her?" He reached behind his back and pulled out a pistol, a compact military weapon with fin-guided, explosive rounds. And pointed it at her. "And to think it was *you*."

She choked up, tried to speak. Nothing came out.

"You remember what I screamed at you, while you hid in my bedroom?"

She swallowed and tried again. "I didn't mean to. You know me, know I'd never—"

"You killed my mother!" His eyes blazed, anger and hatred and hurt given form.

"I know. And I'd change it if I could. I'm so sorry. But Seth, you're not a killer. You're a gentle man, a decent man. You *know* me."

"I do." He pulled the trigger.

SHORTED

Barry couldn't breathe.

He stumbled, dizzy, chest squeezed by a sudden, inexplicable panic. The world hazed from the bustle of a New York City crosswalk to red to black. A creeping, omnipresent dread brought him, shaking and sweating, to the asphalt. Legs bumped against him as the crowd skirted his fetal body, other seventy- and eighty-year-olds rushing to and from jobs as meaningless as their lives.

He crawled on hands and knees toward the shoulder, desperate to get out of traffic before the light turned. The thought of tires crushing his bones and rupturing his organs brought a new wave of panic. Nobody would stop for a Short; he wouldn't have.

Once on the curb he sat back, squeezed his eyes shut against the flashes of sunlight on passing cars, hummed to himself to drown out the rustling shuffle of a million feet like spiders casting webs across his brain.

He forced himself to recall the Professional Development training for dealing with Shorts, a seminar the government required over thirty years earlier after the first chips failed: Shorts may become confused, anxious, irrational. Desperate.

After decades with the regulation chip, they'll be at a loss what to do with a world they find suddenly strange and terrifying, and may become violent. Standing protocol: ignore them, get on with your business, and let the police deal with them.

The police!

They'd picked him up sixty years ago for stealing a car, a stupid act brought about by nothing more than boredom. Compassionate but firm, they'd brought him in and given him his chip, and everything had run like clockwork since. With his help they found—

My sister! He hadn't thought of Sasha since, his moods and concerns regulated by the neural implant. She had had brown hair like his that must have gone gray long ago, and would look just like their mother.

Mama! She couldn't still be alive, not after all this time.

Lying on the curb, he wept for her.

"Why did scientists seed the sky?" Miss Schotts surveyed the room before calling on Barry, to the disappointment of Jayden, who pouted and crossed her arms.

"To increase the albedo of the Earth!" A new word, learned only that day; Barry tasted it on his tongue. Al-bee-dough. A lumpy word, it sounded like a town in Arizona, or a disease that left huge warts all over your skin.

"That's right." His teacher said. "By upping the reflectivity of the upper atmosphere—making it shinier—climatologists like your dad are going to save us all from global warming."

Over the following months, as a way to teach percentages to Barry's fourth-grade class, Miss Schotts had incorporated the numbers into her lessons—0.7 had gone up to 0.76, an increase of 8.57%, made by dispersing reflective nanoparticles into the upper atmosphere. His pride at successful calculation—on paper but without a calculator—locked the numbers into his mind. They followed the results through the months, adjusting their figures on a paper chart Miss Schotts had pinned up next to the Smart Board. Barry got to adjust the chart every day at the beginning of class, his reward for being the son of the man who led the project that would save mankind.

He remembered her frown when 8.57% became 9.2%, her furrowed brow at 10.1%. When they hit 12.8% Barry leaped up onto the stool before the class bell had rung to add more construction paper to the chart, and almost slipped off at the coughing sob that had erupted from the teacher's throat. He turned, tacks in one hand, paper in the other, to find her curled up in her chair, shaking, face buried in her knees. She'd shrieked when Becky tried to comfort her and didn't stop until school security dragged her away—and Barry hadn't missed the wet streaks down the guard's cheeks, either.

On the curb, he kept his eyes squeezed shut and sobbed, unable to contain the anguish of never seeing again the loved ones he hadn't thought about in six decades, unable to process the nightmare world around him, billions of citizens acting out the death throes of human existence until their pointless bodies crumbled to dust. Those years flashed through his mind: punching a clock to shuffle countless medical records for the National Health Board and pass them on to someone else, collecting a check of useless money to pay for an apartment where he sat and watched live feeds of other people doing the same kind of work on his giant television, marking off the days on his electronic calendar because the chip found time important enough to notice, jobs important enough to do. He'd exercised to stay in shape, and for a few decades read United Nations updates on the plight of countries who had refused chipping, until he realized they'd been sending the same recycled updates for at least ten years.

Strong arms wrapped him, and he cried into them, muttering fractal despondencies into their unyielding embrace. They lifted him, set him down on a soft surface.

He opened his eyes when the world jerked. A van, the cab separated from the passenger compartment by a cage. Thick padding covered the floor and walls, the off-white color of clouds choked by smog. Sitting up, he steadied himself on the wall as the driver careened through the streets, barely glimpsed through the window into the passenger's compartment.

Gray hair tumbled in wondrous curls to spill across the padded shoulders of her police uniform, her wizened face a mass of wrinkled, semi-transparent skin. The police had to wear armor because Shorts could turn violent in a moment. The chipped had nothing to gain, but Shorts had nothing to lose; the difference in behavior couldn't be more stark, according to the sixty-something who'd given the lecture. He'd be dead by now, too, his estate turned over to the government for caretaking.

Caretaking for what?

Barry shuddered, consumed by childhood memories no longer filtered through a dispassionate lens built of P-N junctions and microscopic solder joints.

His parents had pulled him out of school, taking Barry and Sasha into the mountains to a home Dad had bought "in case things went wrong." A log cabin on the surface, it had a basement six times bigger than the house, all of it given over to hydroponic gardens and rabbit cages. Sasha had loved the garden, and loved watching wolves and deer and the occasional elk with their father's binoculars, especially the wolves. She worked without complaint but refused to kill rabbits for their meals; his father hadn't spared Barry that kindness. They home-schooled as winter set in early enough to bury crops in California under first inches of snow, then feet. People fled the mountains as the snow piled high, and their father's telescoping rods thrust solar panels ever higher in search of every spare watt.

In the Sierra Nevadas, February stretched into June, and the news spoke of famine, of ships ice-locked in New York Harbor, of mass exodus toward the equator, of bodies piled a hundred high at closed borders. It spoke of hydroponics projects beyond a scale mankind had ever dreamed.

And it spoke of Nyloxx.

Recipients determined by anonymous lottery in the Western world, by fiat elsewhere, the drug would sterilize millions, take pressure off of dwindling resources and give the rest of the human race a fighting chance. A year became two as they ate rabbits and watched old TV shows and learned from books in Dad's library until the day Dad didn't come out of his study. Mom couldn't bring herself to look, and Sasha wouldn't do it, so Barry had put the revolver back in the hidden compartment in the bottom drawer, dragged the body outside where the snow could bury it, and cleaned up the mess—he'd killed and butchered enough rabbits by then that the blood hadn't bothered him, not all that much, and nothing had struggled under his hands.

He cried at night, biting on a finger so they couldn't hear him.

The back door opened to a blast of sunlight, snapping Barry from his reverie. Two blank-faced policemen flanked the driver. Salt-and-pepper hair, good muscle tone, they couldn't have been more than sixty-five. LGs—the last generation.

"Get down, please," one said.

He did, joints aching as he clambered over the bumper and trailer hitch onto the broken asphalt parking lot.

"What's going to happen to me?" It came out a blubbering mess, a tumor of worry unleashed across his mind in an orgy of unwanted emotion. Standing straight, he sniffled, wiped his nose with the back of his hand, and repeated himself in a calmer tone. "What's going to happen to me?"

"Do you understand that your regulator has failed?"

He nodded.

"And that the neural interfaces are too delicate? That once failed it cannot be repaired or replaced?"

Another nod.

"Do you understand that we cannot allow the de-chipped to live among the normal populace?"

He hesitated. For the first time he wondered why; but because he understood the fact, he nodded again.

"We have an area for the de-chipped. You'll not be allowed to leave, but as long as you don't try to escape or commit violence you'll be allowed to stay as long as you like. You'll enjoy all government services uninterrupted."

"Okay." He cast his eyes down and allowed the officers to lead him through the door. It closed behind him, and through the wall he heard the crunch of tires on gravel. He looked up.

Men and women sat at tables in an outdoor yard, watching ancient programs on televisions hung on the walls, or talking in small groups. They ignored him, so he returned the favor to sit at an empty picnic table and wait for whatever would happen to happen.

He hadn't meant to cry, but he wiped away tears and shoved down memories of his family.

As ultraviolet light had pulverized the nanoparticles and the snow melted, survivors drifted back to their homes or dug out from where they'd holed down. A billion people had died, and it would be another several years before crop levels could even hope to return to normal. Nyloxx in genetically-modified food had prevented millions of births, and would prevent billions more if all went to plan. A reduced population could, over time, be managed by the dwindling resources of an exhausted planet.

It took three years for things to return to normal, or a veneer of normal stretched over regret and loss. Barry and Sasha watched the renewed news broadcasts from the safety of their mountain refuge, Barry itching to get out of their icy tomb, Sasha already planning how best to help people. On their TV screen they watched the survivors go back to work, rebuilding their lives as if they hadn't just dodged the apocalypse, as if they hadn't murdered and stolen their way through the Long Winter, as if they hadn't "done what they had to do" at the expense of anything and anyone that got in their way. Billions of monsters fell grateful into banality, seizing the opportunity to forget. Then, given the chance, these people elected the same politicians, who vowed greater oversight over the same scientists, who in turn said they were very sorry and vowed to be so much more careful in the future.

His mother enrolled them in private school, and booked them tennis and golf lessons, and went back to work at the charity, now overseeing the stunning number of orphans created by the savagery of the past half-decade. Barry read and learned and golfed—he had no aptitude for tennis, and no desire to gain one—and with the help of tutors and teachers climbed to the top ten percent of his class. Sasha volunteered at a refugee camp until the day she took a beating for being her father's daughter. They'd broken her nose and bruised her kidney, and six weeks later the sixteen-year-old girl went back, defiant and fearless in her search for a better humanity.

Wood creaked next to him.

"Hi, I'm Janice."

Barry opened his eyes to a face he could have recognized. Wizened, liver-spotted, with papery skin stretched too thin over a freckled skull sporting wisps of yellow-white hair. Her lips pulled back to expose her teeth, an awkward tic on the verge of hideous; it took him a moment to recognize a smile.

"Barry," he said, just able to choke out the word.

She reached out and grabbed his hand. Too stunned to react, he didn't pull away as she flipped it over and ran her fingers down his. Rheumy wetness rimmed her eyes.

"We've met, you know."

He shook his head. "When?"

"Last year, after a meeting with your boss. We shared an elevator, and I shorted on the way down. You left me there on my knees for the police."

He opened his mouth, closed it.

"You don't have to apologize. I rode that elevator for hours before they showed up. You had a lot of company."

"Then how do you remember me?"

"We were talking when it happened."

"I don't—" Only he did remember. She fell on him, screaming and crying, and he'd turned to face the doors. "I'm so sorry."

"You didn't know any better."

He closed his eyes. "But now I do. And I'm sorry."

Crawling under the façade of normalcy, one critical thing had changed. Neonatal wards dwindled and died, their empty halls abandoned or repurposed to other ends. Even a five-year-old could do this math—Nyloxx administered to sixty percent of the population should have reduced new births by sixty percent, not a hundred.

As birthrates collapsed to zero, scientists far too like his father wrung their hands and tried to explain. Words like "systemic" and "persistent" did little to assuage a race faced with their self-caused extinction. Years of research caused eventual pregnancies. They rejoiced along with the rest of the world at the first pregnancy, and thousands more induced with drugs and in vitro fertilization. They cried together at her miscarriage. A second miscarriage followed, then thousands, then millions. In desperation, children carried to twenty-three weeks were extracted via C-section; none survived.

Smothered under the blanket of impending oblivion, many killed themselves, sometimes taking their families with them in poison or car crashes or hot red shotgun blasts, sometimes slipping away alone under the embrace of opiates or narcotics. Some turned to God, reconciling their unanswered prayers with a just punishment mankind must have somehow deserved. For a few years art thrived, turning ever darker before collapsing under the inevitability of the end.

Many wandered, not bothering to bathe or work, shuffling from soup kitchen to park and back. Sasha stayed out later and later as their numbers grew, choking the streets and emptying factories, collapsing production and shifting ever more burden onto those few who would still provide for others. At Barry's behest she gave it up, gnawing at the bit in their solitude, sullen rage spiked by occasional bouts of despondent impotence.

Drugs proved unreliable, for them or for anyone—antidepressants could help with day-to-day anxieties, but held no power over the hopelessness of a world that hadn't seen a live birth in five years. Neuroscientists had discovered a means to artificially suppress or stimulate the amygdala, hippocampus, and other parts of the brain to control emotional response, and the government offered the chip—in reality a network of chips implanted throughout the brain—to anyone who wanted it. Results looked promising, and ever more people signed up until only a few holdouts in any given community refused the treatment.

It didn't take years for volunteer treatment to become mandatory. Unpredictable and violent, the un-chipped presented a danger to civilized society. They had to be treated for the good of all.

Back in their mountain retreat, his mother and Sasha worked with an underground movement to resist forced chipping. Uninterested in their politics and bored of always being cooped up, Barry had run down to the nearest town to score whatever booze he could dig up from the zoned-out chippers' basements, and stole a car to get home. He floored it when a cop drove up behind him, went off the road and hit a telephone pole.

He remembered struggling against their professional insistence—and their handcuffs—up until the moment the needle went into his neck.

And he remembered calmly walking the calm-faced men in suits through how to get to their house, how to disable the security system, and where they were likely to find his mother and sister so that they might calm them, too.

Janice shook her head, chewing and swallowing the bite of her apple before replying.

"No. If you try to escape they'll kill you. They call it 'aggressive noncompliance.' Nobody gets out of here except in a body bag."

"That's absurd," Barry said. Three weeks in "the yard" and he'd managed to go only the past two days without breaking down into hysterical sobbing more than once or twice. He didn't understand these people and their weary resignation, he just knew he had to find his sister.

"There's no such thing as absurd anymore."

"No, I guess not. But if Sasha's alive I have to find her."

Janice smiled, and this time he recognized the beauty in it. Ninety-two years old, she'd been one of the last to give birth to a viable child, a son she'd had chipped at six years old because that's what you did to the un-chipped. He stayed with her until a heart attack took him on his sixty-second birthday ten years earlier; she grieved him suddenly and passionately in an elevator a decade later.

"You can't know she's out there."

"No, but if she were chipped I'd have seen it. I've—I've got a good memory for numbers, always have. Her social security number never came across my desk. Not once, ever."

"It's a big world. You can't have seen them all."

"Two five four, seven six, three one five seven."

A grunt, possible acknowledgement that he'd pulled hers from his memory.

"I'm going home. I know how to get there. I just need to get out of here."

She pinned him with a hard stare. "Aggressive noncompliance."

"There has to be a way."

Her head dropped into her hands. She rubbed her face before looking up at him, fingertips peeling down her eyelids into a gross caricature. "These people are emotionless. Don't you understand what that means?" Sitting up, she grabbed his hands and squeezed them. "They don't get bored or antsy or horny, they don't get distracted. They just guard us and eat and sleep until they die of old age. That's it. They have nothing better to do, because they don't want to do anything else."

"There has to be a way. What about the garbage?"

She quirked an eyebrow. "What do you mean?"

"The trash has to leave here somehow."

"Compactor. Messy."

Hopelessness squeezed his heart. "What, then? There has to be something."

She sighed, long and melodramatic, before letting go of his hands. "Let me talk to some people. There might be a way."

For the first time in his adult life, a glimmer of hope burned in his chest. He closed his eyes.

"Thank you."

The police had come back to him with a report: no sign of his family at the mountain hideout.

He gave them their old address, before the Long Winter, and their new address after, plus his mother's work and Sasha's old daycare provider. A thousand questions later they released him, sent him to training for his new job. He never got an update on them, and until he'd shorted it had never occurred to him to wonder.

Janice ate her canned spaghetti with gusto, slurping the pasta into her mouth to mash it apart with her dentures. Her companions, three men he'd only met in passing but who treated her with old fondness, ate theirs with similar flair. Barry looked down at the limp noodles and runny, pink sauce pooled beneath them, a tomato-and-vegetable-protein derivative he'd eaten countless times without complaint, and his stomach churned.

"You must be hungrier than I am." He pushed the plate away.

Janice pushed it back. "No, no. Eat it, and all of it. Now."

"I'm not hungry."

Her companions scowled. The shriveled, bald man to her left pushed up his thick glasses and stared down his nose at them both. "You didn't tell him, did you?"

"I didn't."

Barry twirled a bundle of soppy noodles onto his fork and shoved them into his mouth. "Told me what?" he said around the wad of pasta.

"We drugged your spaghetti."

He choked, then swallowed.

"What?"

She twirled up another bite. "Romeo and Juliet ploy. You want out, we're getting you out." Another forkful went into her mouth.

"So I'm going into a coma?"

"For a day, maybe two. They never pay much attention to the bodies when they get a mass suicide. Just toss them into a tarpaulin and haul them to the dump. This was basically your idea, so chow down."

"My—mass suicide?" He brightened, and plowed through another forkful. "You're coming with me?"

She patted his hand. "No, dear. We're not coming with you. There's nothing for us out there. We're just …"

"The diversion," the bald man finished for her, slurping up the last noodle and wiping up the last of the sauce with his finger.

"What … what's in your pasta?"

"Ground peach and cherry pits. Should be lethal in … minutes."

A python constricted his chest, his breath staccato explosions that didn't draw in enough air. "You can't! It's—"

Janice coughed, covering her mouth with the back of her hand. Swooning, she fell against the man next to her.

"Wow. Fast." His eyes bugged out in alarm before he slumped forward onto the table.

Barry tried to stand, spun, and landed face-down on the bench. He reached out across the table for Janice's limp hand, but lost consciousness before he touched it.

Darkness.

He fumbled for his light, touched cold flesh, recoiled.

Breath came in panicked jerks, and brought with it the sharp, throat-burning stench of bodily fluids and death. Woozy eddies drowned the world.

Squirming against the slick, stiffened meat of his companions, he lashed out against the thick, rubbery blanket that choked off air and light.

Fingers brushed metal. He followed the rough line, found the edge, and dug his fingernail into it. He gasped as the zipper parted, at the gust of warm, fetid air and the sudden pain in his finger. It pulsed, red in the dying sunlight, the nail pulled back and out of the flesh. He put it in his mouth, sucked on it, and moaned when he looked down, clenching his teeth around the top of his knuckle to muffle the sound.

Four bodies lay in the bag with him, naked flesh slicked with shit and vomit, faces twisted into agonized rictuses frozen in place by rigor mortis. Janet leered at the night sky, dead eyes glittering under the moonlight, toothless mouth a final indignity—the police had taken her dentures along with her clothes. Had his companions killed themselves for him, or had they used him as an excuse to end their wait? Did it matter? He scrambled for purchase, putting his arms on things he didn't want to think too hard about, and pushed, kicking with his legs to free his lower body from the tangle.

Old bones creaked. Withered muscles strained.

His leg came free with a wet sucking noise and he erupted from the bag. The world spun too much to stay on his hands and knees. Gasping, he collapsed face down on the heaped refuse. He wept, for the obvious, callous inevitability of it. The police had dropped their bodies in the dump with the rest of the garbage.

It took a while—minutes or hours, he didn't know—for the world to stop its relentless spin, settling into a queasy knot in his stomach.

He clambered down the mess, past old appliances and furniture, the remains of entire houses and buildings dumped for lack of anything useful to do with them—reduce, reuse, recycle, save the planet, conserve fossil fuels; all of it had been rendered pointless by the Long Winter and the solution to it, Nyloxx, loose in the soil.

Goosebumps pricked at his skin; not the chill of winter but a cool summer breeze across his wet, bare skin. Nose wrinkling at his own stench, he found an old throw pillow and tore off the cover, using the coarse fabric to wipe off the worst of the grime and moist decay.

He pulled a plaid dress shirt and newish jeans from an old dresser and elsewhere scored a pair of black leather dress shoes, but put on none of it. Creeping up under cover of heaped garbage, he tried the door to the trailer by the entrance and found it unlocked; in the age of the regulator, no one had a reason to steal. He let himself in, washed up as best he could in the bathroom sink, and put on the scavenged clothes.

A wraith stared out the mirror. Gray hair wild, chin a riot of scruffy gray whiskers, eyes sunken and haunted. No one would mistake him for chipped, but he didn't have a razor or even a comb.

He wet his hands and patted down his hair, called it good enough, and stumbled out into the night.

He followed the stark white streetlights to town, a mindless little village consisting of a cafeteria and three office buildings surrounded by largely automated farms, their GPS-controlled combines and autoharvesters working in the dark to feed a dwindling populace. Nine cars sat on Main Street, and he had to laugh. An ancient Tesla XVII sat under a light, the streamlined four-seater an updated clone of the model he'd stolen six decades earlier.

A raucous noise echoed down the street, a ragged cry from a throat unused for laughter. He clamped his hand over his mouth. Hurrying before anyone investigated, he opened the door, slipped inside and hammered the button with his thumb. The lights clicked on and a navigation screen overlaid the windshield. He turned it off, preferring the dim quiet, and pulled out onto the road.

He'd never made the drive, and it had been a lifetime, but he knew it by heart. His headlights crawled up the mountain at thirty miles an hour. Sick and weak from whatever the hell Janice had given him, he couldn't trust anything faster. The world still swam when he turned too fast, and with the human population shattered, he expected a million deer to throw themselves in front of his car, but saw none.

He entertained the idea that Nyloxx hadn't poisoned them, too. Maybe wolves had come back, kept the herds in check. Sasha had always loved wolves.

The road deteriorated as deciduous, temperate trees gave way to old-growth conifers, and he had to turn on the heater to keep the windows from fogging. The dark swallowed him, and the rhythm of the wheels rocked him to a lullaby of night sounds. He shook his head to stay awake, rolled down the windows to let in the chill.

At long last he found the driveway, smothered with tall grass tamped down into a pair of overgrown packed-earth runnels. Twin silver lines marred the grass where someone had driven over it in the past few days, or at least since the last rain. He turned and eased down on the gas. The car rolled through with a hiss that increased and decreased in intensity with his speed, interrupted here and there by the sharp bang of a Black-Eyed Susan against the bumper. Mama had planted those flowers in their garden, the year after the snow melted; they'd spread, and now dotted wherever trees hadn't smothered. His mind failed him on how far he had to drive, but he knew the moment before the cabin came into view.

No lights shone in the windows, and moonlight scattered off a roof that jarred with his recollection—slate gray tin instead of mottled brown shingles. The yard had disappeared under a wild green tangle, and the bannister leading up the front steps to the porch lay akimbo next to the disconnected, rotting porch swing.

His spark of hope flickered, dimming to match the vacant cabin.

He killed the car and got out, shutting the door with more authority than was necessary. If anyone lived here, he didn't want them surprised.

A reluctant shuffle dragged him up the creaking steps to the front door. Ajar, it creaked open to reveal the ruined remains of human habitation—a rotted-out couch showing springs and rat's nests; moldy plates piled next to the sink visible through the kitchen door; the old, red-brick hearth blackened and littered with beer cans.

"Hello?" His voice rang out in the empty, soulless space. A fat raccoon darted from under the couch, bumbled two steps toward the door, then retreated into the kitchen without undue haste—it didn't fear him. And why should it? Why should any animal fear man anymore?

With no answer, he approached the bookcase against the far wall. Most of his father's collection had disappeared. A few had rotted to nothing. But *The Book of Daniel* by E.L. Doctorow stood tall and proud on the third shelf up, the sleeve on the hardcover defying the ravages of time, except for a scuff on the spine betraying the aluminum underneath.

He grabbed the book with both hands, pushing in the top while pulling out the bottom. It gave. The bookcase popped away from the wall on silent hinges, revealing the ladder leading below.

The rich, earthy smell of a garden twisted his stomach. His mouth went to sandpaper at the thought of killing another rabbit, cutting around its neck and tearing off its skin moments after petting it and calling it a good girl. He gagged on the memory, sucking in air to displace it—sterile, cool, bleach with a sweet hint of lemon. Someone had cleaned, and recently.

He climbed down the two stories, knees aching with every rung, knuckles white as the vertigo ebbed and flowed. "Hello?" he called, halfway down, voice echoing through the tiny antechamber that led to the greenhouses. His feet hit the floor and he walked through the dark to the light switch, flicking it up with old confidence.

As the LEDs flashed on, figures rushed him. Stars exploded through his skull as they slammed him against the wall, pinning his arms and legs with their bodies.

A black woman in nurse's scrubs looked him up and down, and grunted. Her gray afro matched wrinkled skin stretched over chubby cheeks, the softness in her face at odds with the murder in her eyes. "Shorted, did you?"

"Yes," he said, breath short and raspy through the fingers around his throat.

"It's Esther." She backed up, and his assailants let him go. He rubbed his wrists and stepped away from the wall.

"You know me?"

"Your name is Barry Esther. You must be, what, seventy-four?"

"Seventy-three."

"Seventy-three. I'm Annie, and I'm in charge here. Don't do anything impulsive."

"I won't," he said. "I'm just looking for my family." Her smirk could have meant anything. Hope soared, fragile and exposed. "Are they here?"

"Your mother passed not long after you were taken. Sasha called it a broken heart."

It had to be true. Knowing stabbed an icicle through his chest.

"A long time, then."

"A long time," Annie said. "We have some of her things in Sasha's desk."

"She's here?"

Annie jerked her head toward the door to the greenhouse. "Follow me."

It wasn't an answer, exactly.

One of his attackers, an old man over six and a half feet tall, opened the door into soft, warm light. Barry stepped around the huge man and gasped.

The greenhouse of his childhood shattered into memory, replaced by a hospital ward, two rows of fifty—no—sixty beds. Women lay in each, most of their bellies bulging to one degree or another. IVs trailed upward from needles piercing their arms; skinny legs stuck out from underneath hospital gowns. Gray and wrinkled, the youngest of them couldn't have been ten years his junior. And none of them looked enough like his sister to be an older version of her.

"What is this place?"

"The Nursery. Sasha founded it, not long after, you know. After. We knew each other from the food kitchen, you remember?" He nodded; she continued. "Twenty years in she found me, shorted, administering what care I could to other Shorts. She offered me a chance to do something more."

Annie walked down the rows and he followed, waiting patiently as she passed kind words and greetings to each woman, touching hands and kissing foreheads, rubbing pregnant bellies and massaging swollen feet, until at last she stopped at a small desk set against the farthest wall. Above it sat a portrait of his family, smiling in happier times—he couldn't have been more than five. Barry leaned forward, knees turning to jelly, unable to think, to breathe. They got him settled into a chair and handed him the frame. He ran his fingers down the glass, leaned in and kissed it.

No psychic connection crackled from the smooth, cold surface. No mystic message whispered across time that everything would be all right. He wiped his eyes and looked down at the book, leather-clad with "Sasha Esther" emblazoned in peeling silver on the bottom-right corner. Setting down the photo, he opened the diary, hands shaking.

The first page showed an old printed picture, ink faded with time. Sasha, a beautiful, vibrant woman a mirror of their mother, leaning against a man as she cradled an infant, so tiny, too tiny, his head bulging over his right eye, his left drooping too low. A sad smile blossomed on her loving face. Underneath, it said, "Sasha, Bob, and Little Barry."

He read. With fertility drugs she'd conceived, birthing Barry during C-section at twenty-three weeks. He'd lived three days. Their next lived a week. The one after that miscarried fourteen weeks in, the next bled down her leg after only ten.

Through blurred eyes, he found the nurse.

"Where is she? Can I see her?"

The nurse nodded toward the desk, where a small purple vase rested against the wall. It had shattered and been repaired with gold, an old Japanese trick their father had loved, the beauty that came from broken things. Barry remembered it from Sasha's room, after their father had passed—she'd taken it as a memory of him, and kept flowers in it when she could find them. Now, a crude engraving near the bottom said SME, dated thirty years earlier. He ran his fingers down the smooth pottery, traced the letters.

"She's gone." Like everyone else. "So you put her on a desk?"

"I'm sorry," Annie said. "She wanted to rest with her children."

He swallowed. "What happened?"

"She carried her fifth to twenty-five weeks. We pulled her out, but your sister didn't survive. The baby made it nine days. We named her Ruth."

"Sasha was, what? Fifty-one years old?"

"About that."

"What was she doing having children?"

The nurse stepped back—he still didn't know her name—and gestured at the beds. "Do you see anyone here of childbearing age? Thousands of women have lain in these beds. Tens of thousands. We do what we can: fertility drugs, different donors, in vitro stabilization techniques, genetic engineering. We've had children survive ten days, even two weeks, with so few deformities, hell, you could almost think them normal. It's … progress."

"Have any lived? Beyond … beyond—"

"No. And it only gets worse as their mothers get older. But one of these days we might get lucky."

"Then why?"

She kneeled next to him and whispered into his ear. "What else are we to do?"

A noise escaped his lips that might have been a laugh, might have been a cry of despair.

Barry couldn't breathe.

He stumbled out of the chair, dizzy, his chest squeezed by a sudden panic. Voices, stern and sharp, called out behind him as he rushed for the door. The bookcase creaked shut as he reached the squalid living room, but the python around his chest wouldn't let in any air.

The world hazed from red to black.

He came to at his father's desk, the wood pale and cracked after so many years of neglect. Sasha's urn sat in front of him, the purple and gold vase encasing all that remained of hope or joy, a beautiful lie that things can be repaired, made more beautiful. A million white lines crackled through the glaze, the truth of entropy made manifest on the vessel that contained the ashes of hope. Inert, lifeless. Like the rest of the world.

His father's revolver rested warm in his hands, the black metal marred with flecks of rust where pieces meshed, the faintest smell of gunpowder still lingering in the drawer that lay open at his knee. He'd cleaned it, oiled it, that day long ago, but nothing lasts, no matter the care taken.

He raised it, turned it over, ran his fingers down the dark curves. He cocked the hammer, and it slid back with little difficulty, latching into place with a faint click.

Outside, a wolf howled.

Tears melded the urn into the gun, the gun into the urn. Sasha had always liked wolves.

He pressed cold metal against his temple. The trigger rubbed rough against his index finger.

A second wolf answered the first. Then a third, and a fourth.

His father's pistol rang in reply.

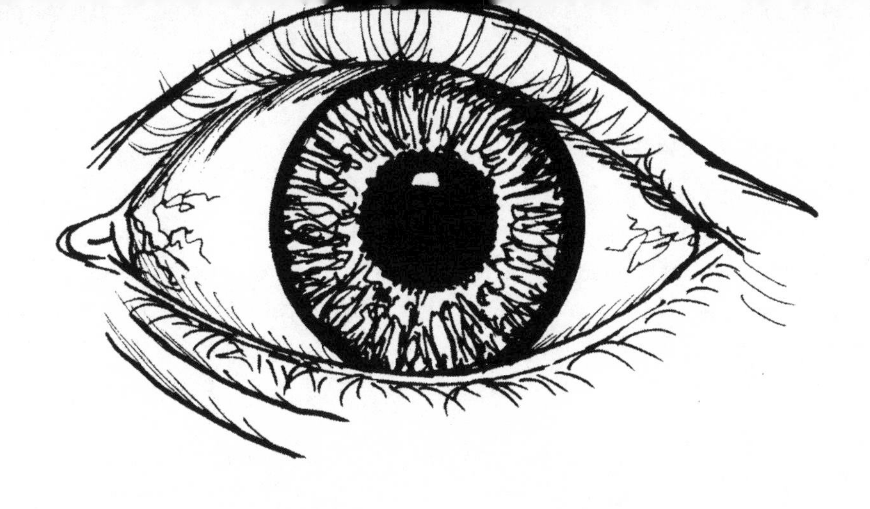

SNAPSHOT

Liz hissed as her pregnant belly touched the cold marble sink. She brushed back a lock of auburn hair, spat out her toothpaste, and rinsed the cloying mint taste from her mouth. She stepped back from the vanity and frowned.

"You look beautiful," Scott said, squeezing in behind her and sliding his arms up under her shirt to her abdomen. "Just thinking about this … I love you!"

She grunted. "I look like a bloated hippopotamus."

"A beautiful, bloated hippopotamus." Scott grinned at her in the mirror, flashing perfect white teeth in a perfect, rugged face crowned with perfect blond hair. The star anchor of *Rise and Shine America* always looked perfect before he left the house. Hell, he looked perfect with bed-head and a five-o'clock shadow.

She closed her eyes and leaned back into him. "I'm just ready to be done with all this. I'm tired and fat and tired of being fat."

His hands slid upward and squeezed her breasts. They were swollen and tender, and his hands rough, but she didn't stop him. He whispered in her ear. "A couple weeks. You'll be back in bikini shape in no time."

She smiled as he nibbled her ear, and craned her neck as his lips moved lower. She turned around and kissed him, long and hard.

She nibbled his lip, then bit a little harder. She pressed against him, inhaling his scent, but when his hands slid lower she shoved him back into the wall. "None of that, now. You need to get to work." She stole another kiss and then darted into the hall, dancing as best she could from his grasping hands.

It took Liz an hour to get comfortable. She frowned at Scott, untroubled by the burden of childbearing, fast asleep with his arms over his head, an Adonis in repose. She closed her eyes and the world faded to darkness, and then to peace.

A pitiful cry split the night. Liz groaned and groped across the bed. Her arm found a shoulder and she shook it. "Honey." He didn't respond. She shook harder. "Scott!" She cracked an eyelid. He hadn't budged. "It's your turn."

Scott ran his tongue over his teeth. "Okay." He sat up, rubbed his eyes, and stood. "Yeah, um … I got it." He shuffled into the hall. She heard him murmur in the next room, and the wails turned to quiet sobs. She rolled onto her back. *Damn it, now I have to pee.*

She struggled to her feet and shuffled to the bathroom. A minute later she stepped into the nursery. Scott sat on the bed, cradling their three-year-old daughter in his arms. She blubbered around a thumb jammed between her teeth, her head a riot of tangled blonde hair.

As Liz leaned against the door, Josie lifted her head. "Mommy?" Her brittle voice cracked, and her pale green eyes stared outward, unseeing in the lamplight.

"Yeah, sweetie. Mommy's here."

Josie held out her arms, grasping at the air. Scott stroked her head, but didn't let her go. Liz tiptoed across the cold wooden floor. Her knees ached as she knelt and rubbed her daughter's leg. Josie grabbed her head with both hands and hugged her cheek to cheek.

Josie's voice was a bare whisper. "It hurts, Mommy. A lot."

"I know, baby. I'm sorry."

Josie chocked back a sob. "It really—"

Liz shushed her, patting her head as her eyes rolled to Scott.

"Did Daddy give you medicine, sweetie?" She felt the answering nod against her cheek. "Do you want to sleep with us?" Josie nodded again. "Okay. Daddy's going to take you."

Once situated in their bed, Josie's pain-wracked breathing relaxed to a soft snore. Liz stifled tears of her own.

Scott rubbed her stomach. The baby kicked and he gave her a reassuring smile. "Don't worry. Everything's going to be fine."

She kissed his lips, then stroked her daughter's hair. "I hope so."

Josie grabbed her arm and held it, still asleep, as Liz slipped into a memory.

Josie, just over two years old, pouted in a paper gown. She rubbed her eyes, and Liz pulled her hands from her face.

"Don't rub, sweetie. You'll get puffy."

The pout turned to tears. "Ouchy, Mommy."

"I know it's ouchy," Liz said, tousling her hair. "That's why we're at the doctor."

The door opened and Doctor Schrock stepped through, his eyes glued to the transparency in his hand, his wizened brow furrowed. He gave Josie a perfunctory glance, then put the slide on the light panel mounted on the wall. He flipped a switch, backlighting the picture.

Josie stopped blubbering and looked at the image. Liz recognized the human eye, parts of it anyway. Lens, retina, the big squishy white part. Without preamble, Schrock's finger stabbed an area behind the eye, a squid-looking thing in ugly grayscale.

"Do you know what this is?"

Liz shook her head. Josie copied her.

"This is your daughter's optic nerve. Do you see these gray areas? These black specks?"

She nodded.

"A healthy optic nerve would be all white. Stark white." He poked at the image again. "This? This is troubling."

Her heart caught in her throat. "Troubling?"

"Yes, troubling. More spots on her retinas, see?" Liz didn't see them, but she didn't interrupt. "They're signs of bilateral necrotic neuropathy." He held

up a hand, cutting off her unasked question. "It means the nerves in her eyes are dying."

Liz looked from the specialist to her daughter and back.

"What? I mean … How? Why?"

Doctor Schrock shook his head. "The pathogenesis is unknown. Common causes: acute papillitis, ischemia, or herpes simplex. None of these are present in your daughter's case. There doesn't appear to be a bacterial or viral component."

Liz dropped to her knees and looked in Josie's eyes. Pale green, beautiful, full of life. Perfect. Josie smiled at her, unaware. She looked at Doctor Schrock.

"What does this mean? For her?" She squeezed her daughter tight.

The doctor frowned. "Pain, which is partly treatable with medication, NSAIDs and the like. Blindness, which is not."

Liz gasped. "No. No, not my baby." Images of white canes and dogs and dark sunglasses flooded her mind. "Not my baby …"

Schrock's frown deepened. "I'm sorry. There's little we can do."

She clutched Josie and cried as Doctor Schrock walked out. He left the door open.

Scott was in the shower by the time she woke. Josie lay curled in the fetal position, her thumb in her mouth, her hair scattered across the pillow. Liz leaned over and kissed her temple.

Josie's eyes fluttered open, unfocused and useless. "Hi, Mommy."

"Good morning, baby." Liz stroked her hair. "It's time to get up. Daddy has to work, and you have a doctor's appointment."

As Josie guided herself to her room, one hand on the wall and the other out in front of her, Liz looked at the calendar on the night-stand. Her due date was two weeks away. It seemed like forever.

By the time she got to the breakfast nook, Scott was gone. A vase on the table held a dozen roses, the bouquet lined with baby's breath and green cellophane. Scott's severe handwriting filled the blank card with two words: *Just because.*

She grabbed a tissue to dab tears from her eyes, swiped a Slim Fast from the fridge, and waddled back up the stairs. Josie's shirt was right-side out, but it clashed with her shorts. "Wrong shirt, baby. Let's get you changed."

Liz gasped as the contraction faded. She tried to remember her breathing, but it wasn't easy doing eighty in a thirty-five. Scott swerved around a mail truck into oncoming traffic, then ducked back into the right lane.

"Hold on, girls. We're almost there." He blew through another stop sign.

Gasping, Liz replied. "Honey, you're going to get us killed. It's not that—" She gritted her teeth as the next contraction gripped her. She realized she was holding her breath, and gasped instead. It passed. "Your daughter is in the car."

Scott glanced at Josie in the rear-view mirror, her knuckles white as she clutched the door handle. He slowed to fifty.

"Thank you," Liz said.

They screeched to a halt in front of the blue EMERGENCY sign. Two attendants helped her out of the car as Scott hoisted Josie onto his hip. They put Liz onto a gurney, its front left wheel squeaking as they hurried down the hall. Liz saw the obstetrics sign, and under it a smiling Doctor Faliha in a severe white skirt-suit.

"How often?" Faliha's voice was cheerful as always.

"Every couple minutes," Scott said.

She smiled at Liz. "Well, we'll be done in no time, then." She brushed Josie's cheek with her knuckles. "Go with Valerie, dear. She'll take you to the room where we keep the toys. Get you a drink and some cookies." Scott passed their daughter to the waiting orderly.

Liz heard Josie reply as they wheeled the gurney through the door. "Cookies!"

Liz had never seen so much blood. Josie hadn't been like this. Messy, yes, as all births were, but not so … red. She felt weak, and thanked God the epidural clonidine blocked most of the pain. The contractions were distant, suppressed, and Lamaze was easier. *Soon.*

She pushed, and pushed again. Gritting her teeth, she gasped against the dulled agony and a great relief flooded her. A tiny cry pierced the sterile air. She sighed, exhausted, as Faliha cut the umbilical cord. Scott, ever the trooper, took the baby himself and brought it up so she could see. Even covered in blood and squirming, it had a thick head of auburn hair and a healthy pink complexion.

Liz stared into startlingly blue eyes, and smiled.

"Perfect."

Scott passed the bundle to a male nurse, who swaddled it in a blue fleece blanket and wiped its face. He frowned as the baby grabbed his finger.

Doctor Faliha barked an order. "Take it to Mendel in Harvesting and get it tagged." The nurse nodded and left, the birthing suite door flapping behind him. She turned to Liz. "How do you feel?"

Liz bit her lip, thinking. "Good. Sore, but good."

Faliha stripped off her gloves and dropped them into the biohazard bag. "Excellent. It should be a short recovery. I'll inform Doctor Schrock. He'll be down in a bit."

As she left, Scott grabbed Liz's hand. "You did good, babe." He gave it a gentle squeeze. "Real good."

The squealing children made up for talent with enthusiasm. Josie had spent the afternoon running around with the other children, lost in the joy of play, and with some effort on the part of the parents they had all settled down at the picnic tables. As the last, discordant gasps of Happy Birthday faded to oblivion, Josie puffed her cheeks and blew out the four candles atop the princess cake. One stayed lit, but a second breath snuffed it.

Josie tore into her presents, posing for the camera with each new gift. Uncle Max herded the three of them into a pose, snapped the shot, and showed the screen to Liz. Scott, tall and handsome with a sexy ruggedness that any woman would envy. Liz, fit and trim, beaming at her daughter. Josie, mouth open wide with excitement, looked straight at the camera with her baby blue eyes. Perfect

TRIGGER WARNING

Tom slipped across the ruined plaza

quad this is grass not pavement it's a quad

eyes down, hidden behind dark glasses polarized to reduce glare. Automatic weapons crackled in the distance

dammit just a motorcycle you used to ride one remember there's no threat here

almost too far away to hear. He skirted the burned out tank,

fountain look at it read the inscription it's a fountain

feet shuffling under the weight of the ALICE pack,

books are heavy there's a math test tomorrow there is no threat here

straps cutting into his shoulders through the uniform.

He took shelter in the mosque's

library

entrance, letting the shadows pool around and hide him from the midday sun. He closed his eyes and took a deep breath almost devoid of gasoline and gunpowder and held it, savoring the hint of jasmine and patchouli leftover from some pre-war bazaar.

or the coed smoking three feet away

Fuck it. Orders are orders and

my last order was a big mac there is no threat here

the squad needs cover.

Tom opened his eyes and scanned the burned-out husk

intact buildings

of the town—

campus

He squeezed them shut again and pressed his palms to his temples. Something had gone wrong, something terrible, and he couldn't keep his thoughts straight. He needed

pills like right now isn't soon enough it's been a week

to get upstairs before the squad got into position. If they tried to advance without cover the hajis would take them apart.

Three steps brought him inside the building, into an alcove gaudy with plaster scrollwork defiled by illegible graffiti under a broken bulb. An imam with a great gray beard looked up

she can't be more than twenty she's not a threat

and looked back down at the huge tome without reaction—his mistake. Tom slid left, toward the stairs, grunting in surprise at the flickering exit sign. *How do they have electricity*

come on man it's even in english it says "exit" not جورخ

why would it say that

with the whole grid bombed to shit?

The door opened without protest, revealing a black iron staircase leading up and down. He'd made it up two floors when a group burst onto the next landing, their raucous chatter

that's english not arabic they aren't threats

inappropriate for a place of quiet and introspection. He cut through the lower door into some kind of library, right into the path of a dark-skinned man in a red turban

the red sox don't make turbans that's a ball cap

and blue jeans.

Tom silenced him with a finger strike to the throat, then stepped in and swept the man's legs from under him, cradling him on the way down to muffle the noise. Eyes wide, he had no chance to struggle as Tom slit his throat with a k-bar. The angry red line bubbled and frothed as air escaped from lungs filling with blood. He tried to ignore the tears, put his knife above the heart and leaned in—even jihadis didn't deserve to suffer like that.

He dragged the corpse into the stacks, withdrew the knife. A spurt of blood, a last vestige of fading pressure, soaked into the flannel shirt

> why would a mujahidin wear plaid flannel he was not a threat

in an angry, sad splotch. Tom fondled the steel watch on the man's wrist, somehow out of place, but noise from the stairwell pulled his attention that way.

He held his breath.

The group from above passed by in a wall of guttural chatter,

> they're talking about the voice that's tv not jihad

then paused at the lower landing. Tom grimaced at the corpse's stench, iron and shit and body odor. He preferred the crow's nest, the recoil. The distance.

He looked down at the bloody mess

> there's nothing there you need your meds there is no threat here

and frowned. If someone found it .... Too late. Done is done.

The door clicked shut below, muffling the conversation further. Tom peered out the tiny window, screened between the panes with wire mesh. *All clear.* He took the next four flights three stairs at a time, knees burning by the time he reached the top. Gasping soft, short breaths, he listened for any signs of movement.

In the distance a speaker blared, a crackling recording of a muezzin

> two strokes it's afternoon it's a bell two strokes there is no threat here

calling the faithful to their prayers. *Is it Friday?* Dhuhr on Friday would mean dozens of hajis converging on the temple, everyone but the sentries and what few women remained in the war zone.

He realized he didn't know, and in the end it didn't matter. He had a job to do, and it wouldn't do itself.

He tried the knob. It rotated down a fraction of an inch, then stopped.

Dammit.

He wiggled the k-bar between the door and the frame. A twist, a slide, a fraction of an inch. He repeated the motion, again and again, cursing every lost moment. He exhaled in relief when the deadbolt slipped free, and yanked the door open.

No time to lose.

He kicked the door closed, locked it, and looked up. The ladder stretched another thirty feet, to the top of the minaret,

bell tower

ablaze under the midday sun. He pulled himself up, panting with worry. He'd taken too long. The gunfire

traffic

rose to a crescendo.

He shrugged out of the ALICE pack. He lifted the flap as it hit the plain concrete floor, a ledge just big enough to accommodate him. The black metal, cool to the touch, came together with brutal efficiency. Someone would see the .50 cal stick out the window. An RPG, or a well-placed shot, and that'd be it. But the unit needed him.

He tried the frosted window, but it had been sealed shut. He pried at it as precious seconds ticked by. *No time, no time.*

no threats there are no threats here

He drove the heel of his combat boot into the window. The glass budged. He did it again. Again. A crack appeared, blue sky and contrails. Again. The glass gave way and the view spread out before him. He swallowed. Hundreds of fighters swarmed the town,

afternoon classes it's two o'clock you have recitation now

well more than intel had predicted. A trap.

He pulled the Mk 323 ammunition from the bag, polymer-coated metal in a dozen ten-round box magazines. *Was it enough?*

too much there are no threats here

He lay still, took a breath, positioned the weapon, opened his eyes.

He looked through the scope and gasped, his calm shattered. Jennie lay on the grass, between a young man with a scraggly red beard and a cute brunette. His sister brushed back a lock of blonde hair and laughed at something he couldn't hear. He squeezed his eyes shut.

No, no, not this not now. He knew he was sick. He knew that. But he couldn't let that put his squad in danger. Sergeant Broud said he wasn't at home, had cleared him for action. He had a

math test tomorrow

duty. He took a breath and opened one eye.

The three sentries lounged in the open, the one in the middle a mass of scar tissue masquerading as man. *Bomber. Priority target.*

He put his finger on the trigger, centered the crosshairs below the neck, in the center of the white robe. Body armor couldn't stop this. He exhaled, long and slow.

there is no threat here

yes there is

Jennie rolled onto her stomach and the girl next to her swatted her shoulder. Playful.

The burned man

Jennie that's your sister she is not a threat

did pushups while his companions laughed, a fish in a barrel

she made breakfast this morning eggs and toast and coffee

unaware of the death that awaited her. *Her?*

Him.

Tom blinked. Shook his head. Blinked again. *What the—?*

He looked through the scope.

Jennie grinned,

That's not your sister, that's a target. Take him. Broud cleared you for duty.

rummaged in her bag and produced a pack of gum

Bomb. That's a man with a bomb and he's going to kill your friends.

gum dammit gum not bomb she's chewing it you can't chew a bomb you need your meds you have a test tomorrow there is no threat here

His finger tightened on the trigger.

SPLINTER

She remembered the men, the saws and the smoke and screaming agony and bleeding sap. She remembered the darkness, when they took her and stripped her and killed her and shaved her down to cruel planks. She remembered the darkness, the tepid warehouse harsher than any winter, and the brief kiss of sunlight before her imprisonment.

But she didn't remember before. The dappled sunlight through the forest, squirrels scrambling through her boughs, the deer resting in her shade, the rabbit warren under her roots. She knew these things, but she couldn't remember them.

Brutal geometry stole her form, a giant kiln her essence, mankind her purpose. Jagged steel screws bound her to dead sisters, gave her a form both alien and hostile. Wrapped in cold vinyl and fiberglass and sheetrock, she hardened, stiffened, became as bone to this new thing, this monstrosity, this structure. Eyes of glass saw nothing but her sisters' torture, and concrete roots drew no water to slake her thirst.

She woke to the sound of fawns, human fawns, playing and squabbling and scratching her hardwood floors with their toys. She ached to touch them and feel their warmth, to shelter them beneath her boughs. But she had no shade, no boughs to share, only stone and tar and plaster-covered darkness and the pain of the mill.

They filled her halls with laughter, but she felt only longing. Their plastic games and digital toys left her starved and wanting. Asphalt shingles kept her from the sun, and PVC pipes wouldn't share their water. But as the maples pumped sap into their boughs and buds formed on the willows, she drew upon a hidden strength.

A branch, devoid of leaves or bark, shuddered free from the floorboard. Another followed, and another. She drew the wood into herself, shaping it into a mockery of the fawns bickering in the house below.

She opened new eyes, neither glass nor wood. A splinter of what she once had been, a shard split from a remembered limb, she pried herself from the plank and stood on two wobbly legs. The house sighed in commiseration as she shivered in the dusty, flat, unmoving wilderness of dry cold and old cardboard boxes.

She crept to the half-door and ran gnarled, jagged fingers over a plastic Christmas tree half-stuffed into a tattered box, its nylon needles bright green in defiance of the arid darkness. She jerked back and bared jagged, wooden teeth that sliced her long, purple tongue. The tang of blood—not sap—mingled with the musty, dusty, forgotten smell of the half-full attic. Her elbow brushed against something, and she turned.

She commanded the box fan not to fall, but the plastic rectangle defied her will as no acorn would have dared.

Bob looked up from his newspaper as Nancy dumped scrambled eggs onto his plate. He loved her "Bitchin' Kitchen" apron even though too much time spent in it had allowed her ass to grow too big for her "comfortable" jeans. She stopped mid-scoop, the gelatinous, yellow-orange protein poised to leap from the green spatula.

She scrunched her forehead, prompting a question.

"Well?" The newspaper drooped in the absence of his attention. "What is it, dear?"

"Did you just hear something?"

Between the Saturday morning cartoons and the boys arguing

over their toys, he wouldn't have heard a shotgun blast to his skull. So he shrugged. "Nope."

"You didn't hear something crash upstairs?"

He shook his head and looked back at the paper.

"Bob." Her exasperated sigh grated through his mind and strangled his contentment. "Probably another squirrel in the attic." His restful morning over, he set down the paper and dragged himself to his feet. Once standing, he couldn't escape the honey-do list. "I'll check it out."

Catching a squirrel is impossible, especially in an attic full of eight years of accumulated family junk they hadn't and would likely never unpack. Maybe he could terrorize the rodent into leaving and seal up whatever hole it had found. He loved their new home, but they didn't build them like they used to.

Light washed in from the hallway as the half-door opened, and motes of dust danced above the fallen box fan. She crouched back into the shadows as the male crawled inside the attic, a bristled stick in one hand. She sneered as he called out in sing-songy human sounds unlike anything in the forest. Blood dribbled through her lips.

The man froze, head cocked, like a deer spooked by a rustle in the autumn leaves. He turned toward the door as a gobbet of blood fell from her chin to patter on the floor. He whipped his head toward her and crept forward, knees pounding on the naked plywood.

Desperate to hide, she touched the beam next to her and melded into it. The house absorbed her, silencing her shriek before it left her dry, chemically-impregnated lungs. She struggled and cried out in silence, but it wouldn't let her go, so she wept.

Bob reached down and ran a finger over the red spot on the floor. He held it up and sniffed. The stupid rodent had hurt itself.

Twenty minutes of fruitless searching later, he left the attic. Covered in dust, he walked to the hardware store for advice on squirrel-proofing.

Spring turned to summer's heat, fought off by the unfeeling machinery in her stone roots. Fall turned to winter, and the warmth of flame on air kept her semi-conscious throughout the snows. She dreamed of leaves swaying in the summer breeze, of squirrels and chirping birds, but she felt only the cold darkness that wasn't cold enough.

The fawns, larger now, filled her halls with laughter and squabbles, and as the maples outside pumped sap into their boughs and buds formed on the willows, she woke again. She wouldn't make the same mistake. This time she'd grow.

She stroked the tiny bump on the side of her head, cooed to it, enticed it toward its inevitable potential. It responded to her voice, a whisper of the promise of spring.

As she stepped through the attic door, the wood tried to take her back, where the domineering human spirit demanded that she belonged. Careful to touch only the metal handle, she pushed it closed. The hinges creaked, but she bore them no mind. The adults worked outside to impose human order on grass and shrubs, while the fawns sat enraptured by the electronic sounds and pictures of their game.

She crept into the younger fawn's closet and waited. The passing of a day meant nothing to the passage of long years she knew but couldn't remember, nothing to the passage of the past year, where she burned with the knowledge that she could and would grow again. She shuddered in anticipation, and clutched the tiny acorn growing at her temple. It needed sunlight, and water, but it also needed rich humus and potent soil to grow strong and tall. It needed life.

It took all her will not to coo and sing to the acorn. It needed her voice, but the plan required her silence. If she could wait, so, too, could it. At last the day ended and the fawn slept in its bed, cocooned under cloth-wrapped plastic tendrils and the shredded, entangled remains of her cotton sisters.

The boy gasped as she leapt on him, long black thorns piercing his lungs and throat and limbs. He shuddered and gasped out a last, gargling breath, hot and wet. When he lay still, she wrapped the body in blankets and carried it outside, past endless rows of homes and paved dirt and electric lights, into the starving remains of the forest.

Her glade had disappeared, replaced by tortured bones and oil and stone. She would create a new one.

Singing under the susurrus of a bright moon, she scraped leaves from the ground and dug into the soil beneath. Deep enough, she unwrapped the body, stripped it, and stuffed it into the hole. First leaves, then a little soil.

With trembling hands, she plucked the acorn from her temple, cooed and sang to it, breathed herself into that beautiful potential, and placed it into the bloody mass. The fawn's life would meld with the remnants of hers and produce a new beginning, a sapling. The rest of the soil went on top, then a scattering of leaves.

She couldn't let them find the acorn, so she carried the blankets deep into the woods and stuffed them into a crevasse in the ravine. Unable to contain herself, she scampered back to sing to her spirit, to infuse it with life so that she might grow again. As darkness turned to dawn, she crept back to the house to wait.

Men dressed in blue came in white steeds with angry red, flashing eyes. They banged through her halls and stone roots, they searched the forest. They brought dogs, but she sang to them and told them of her sorrow and pain, and they defied their masters and found nothing.

The days within filled with weeping and rage, with somber gatherings of humans she did not know. She cared nothing for them, only for the acorn and what it would become. Each night she crept to the glade and sang and cooed and cajoled, and its tiny voice joined with hers in the sweetest harmony.

A month passed. Two. Spring turned to summer as they sang together. Summer became fall. The humans left, and took their boxes and furniture and scent with them. The house fell dark with no one to light it, and worry crept into her songs. As the first chill of frost bit the air, she dug in the glade.

She lifted the crumbling, rotten acorn in her hand, disbelief and loneliness her only thoughts, and the forest quaked with her despair. Had she not sung? Did it not have rain and sun and rich soil? Had she imagined its tiny voice, calling to her as she sang, entwining with hers in the harmony of new life?

She fled to the house, cold and unfeeling and empty, and ran to the attic. She found the beam and dove into it, melding and becoming one with her prison. Her loss consumed her through the frigid winter months, cold but not cold enough.

In the darkness of February, humans visited. A few at a time, always with the same woman, with hair the color of beech bark. They talked, a cacophony of goose sounds, and toured the empty home. A family moved in, a man and a woman with a small boy fawn, and filled her with noise and life.

As maples pumped sap into their boughs and the willows budded, she realized the truth. She stood in the attic and fingered the acorn on her elbow, tiny and green and full of promise and joy. No longer a tree, she didn't have the strength to breathe into it, couldn't give it what it needed.

One hadn't been enough. Not enough life, not enough blood. She'd need them all.

In the attic darkness she sat and cooed and whispered, and waited for night.

EARL PRUITT'S SMOKER

"Earl Pruitt died."

Jamie Schwaeble froze, forkful of hash browns halfway to her mouth, ears pricked to catch the rest of the old man's pronouncement. A mainstay at church each Sunday, Pruitt and his wife had kept to themselves despite generous annual donations to the congregation.

"His wife found him last evening, next to some of those hives of his."

"Was he allergic?" His companion, the square-jawed man who worked the counter at the auto parts store, darted a glance at Jamie, from her face to her chest and back up. She turned away, flushing, and buttoned the top of her blouse to hide the glimpse of white T-shirt beneath.

"No," the older man continued. "Been stung a million times and never had a problem. Must have been his heart, or his brain."

"At his age? Could have been anything."

Their conversation wandered from the weather to plans for Vacation Bible School but came back to Pruitt, and the auction his widow planned to make up for their lack of life insurance.

Goosebumps shot up Jamie's arms, a tingle of excitement she shared with, she was sure, a hundred other people. The reclusive old beekeeper never let anyone on his property, a fenced-off farm on the far edge of town that boasted who knew how many bee hives scattered around the barns and outbuildings just visible from the road. The thought of getting a taste of what he kept inside, maybe even picking up a little something, brought a flush of heat to her cheeks.

Pastor Carr would have something to say about such feelings, as he did about any feelings that didn't keep a soul on the narrow, straight path to Heaven. She'd trembled under the weight of his words, one with the hundreds of sinners to bow down at his church each Sunday, and if he were here he'd see the excitement on her face and ask her, and she'd tell him, and he'd admonish her for her sinful desires. She turned back to her food, grateful for her corner booth where the old men and young men couldn't tempt her with their knowing looks and their lustful smiles. She wanted those smiles, and the promises behind them, and knew that wanting them was as wrong at twenty-two as it had been at fourteen.

She paid her bill and fled home to her lonely single-wide, all she could afford on a retail salary but enough to escape the stifling attentions of her stepfather and his son.

Guilt knotted her insides, twisted and pulled at her conscience the rest of the week, castigating her for her weaknesses. But the next week she drove to Pruitt's farm, through the main gate and onto the parcel of lawn now dedicated to parking. Her turtleneck and loose-fitting jeans hid her body from leering eyes, so she hoped the Lord would forgive her a touch of eyeshadow, a tiny rose of blush. Pastor Carr had called beekeeping a vocation suitable for a young woman who had not yet found a husband, a holy calling as old as the New Covenant itself.

Hundreds of people milled around, most of them old bearded beekeepers in denim and fraying flannel. License plates on their vehicles said everything from Georgia to Montana to Maine, but they talked like neighbors as they surveyed the equipment, slapping their hands with battered, wrinkled checkbooks. Some had brought flatbed trucks and forklifts in anticipation of going home with something worth the trip, while others spoke of U-Hauls should the need arise. She hovered around them, another group she could join but never quite become a part of.

Jamie had read of the dangers of used woodware, most especially the specter of American Foulbrood destroying her girls and every honeybee colony within flying distance, so she avoided even the so-called "nuc boxes"—half-sized chipboard containers built to hold starter colonies. Cost and practicality kept her from bidding on the larger equipment—centrifugal extractors, chain uncappers, and other esoteric machines of great use to large commercial operations but far too much for a clerk with one hobby colony she'd owned for less than a season. Even if she could have afforded them, a lack of time and space prevented her from considering the live colonies, grouped as they were in five-pallet blocks, four hives on each, each lot starting at two thousand dollars.

She stopped cold, frozen in place by a table heaped with Pruitt's personal equipment. A dozen beekeeping books, including a first edition Richard Taylor with a reserve of $100, hive tools and other widgets and bobbins piled into musty cardboard boxes held together with little more than duct tape and hope. She fingered through several of the books, interesting for their historical perspective but of little use in the age of varroa mites, GMO crops, and neonicotinoid pesticides; she'd have bought them all if she'd had the money.

Someone cleared their throat, drawing Jamie's gaze.

Mrs. Pruitt sat off to the side as strangers poked through her late husband's things, modestly dressed in a New York Giants sweatshirt, faded jeans, and dusty brown cowboy boots. Her white hair shone almost blue under the summer sun, and webs of old, dark blood crackled under her papery, liver-spotted skin. The childless widow wore a tight-lipped, mirthless smile, a mask of propriety against the lonely cruelty of a life ended, a seventy-three-year marriage that wouldn't see seventy-four. The ancient woman watched for a while, then retired behind the hard wood of her farmhouse door to let her lawyer and the auctioneer handle the rest.

Jamie rummaged, and an electric thrill jolted up her spine at the ancient hive smoker buried beneath a pile of comb-cutting equipment. Just smaller than a coffee can, the weathered tin sported a small dent near the bottom, but otherwise appeared to be in good shape. Several layers of metal reinforced the crimp holding the cylindrical body in place. In lieu of rivets, hot-bent pegs held the polished wood handle and supple leather bellows to the fire chamber, a soot-crusted cylinder that smelled faintly of pine sap and char. The wire cage around the fire chamber had black flecks around the soldered joinings, but held firm when she tapped it with a finger. A single Phillips-head screw held the perforated metal an inch above the air chamber, the only nod to post-1920 technology, an unwelcome stainless-steel concession to the ravages of time and entropy.

It hummed in her hands, a beautiful example of late-nineteenth century metalwork, solid and practical like the country folk it had been built to serve. She entertained the possibly that Moses Quinby himself may have made it hundreds of miles to the east in the Hudson Valley, a personal tool for personal use before his invention spread across the world.

She searched for a maker's mark, and found none.

Jamie glanced around to see if anyone else had noticed, then stuffed the smoker back under the junk in the box and joined the crowd waiting to bid on each lot. The auctioneer started small to milk the most he could out of the cheaper items. She passed on the initial lots, but perked up at the first of the cardboard boxes. Bidding started at two dollars. Her heart leaped into her throat when she took it for nine.

She rushed home with her prize, not quite able to outrun a twinge of guilt at the score.

Dumping the comb-cutting equipment onto the picnic table, she scooped up the smoker. With a little dryer lint for kindling and a few twigs, she pumped the bellows until a rich gray puff launched from the nozzle, then popped it open and added a handful of small twigs. It shut with a satisfying snap, the fit still perfect after so many years. She went back to pump it a few more times while dressing in her crisp white bee suit and mesh veil, until a heavy white cloud rose over her home.

A trail of wood smoke followed her to her single colony. An earthy mélange like cloves and allspice mingled with the sharp tang of the smoldering twigs, a heady mixture reminiscent of fresh cookies baking on a cool spring day. She breathed it in, held it, savored the faint burn in her lungs, the warm, homey taste on her tongue. She'd always loved the smell of smoke, another tally Pastor Carr put against her soul.

Worker bees took off from the landing board at twenty miles an hour and came back heavy with nectar, or with their legs laden with pollen in bright forsythia yellow and pale jasmine violet. A few guard bees peered at her from the long, narrow slit of the bottom entrance, and a few more from the hole drilled halfway up the top super. Vigilant, watchful, but not yet hostile. She sent a light whisper of smoke to the hole, scattering them, then leaned down and doused the entrance with a heavy trio of puffs.

The billowing cloud enveloped her, a hundred times more intense. A hot rush enveloped her like the dark throes of the Passion, and her vision blurred. The world became indistinct, her body light as a feather under the warmth of the summer sun. Head swimming, she put a hand out to steady herself on the hive's metal outer cover, and it vanished in the smoke.

The acrid tang of burning wood gave way to the warm beeswax scents of vanilla and honey and a million summer flowers, intermingled with the chemical communication of tens of thousands of honeybees. A gasp escaped her lips, the noise drowned by the hum of countless wings. A myriad of insects made into one glorious whole, Jamie rose up, out of the garden, her consciousness expanding with the whirling storm of pheromones to where the drones darted and raced in their ceaseless quest to end their lives in a coital explosion with a virgin queen. Everywhere at once, she flitted from blossom to blossom, sucking up sweet nectar into her honey stomachs, or stuffing precious pollen into the baskets on her legs. She foraged water to cool the hive, extending her proboscises to lap dew from fallen leaves on the forest floor or the drips from the leaky sprinklers in the vegetable garden next door.

In the hive she raised larvae, feeding nectar and pollen and just the right amount of royal jelly to make them strong enough to serve the hive but keep them forever juveniles so that they might never challenge the queen. She dragged the dead out the front entrance, larvae or workers who succumbed to the constant threats of bacteria, viruses, poison, mites. She built comb, reaching down to countless abdomens to pull from the glands there, white wax as pure as snow and not yet stained by the tracks of her million feet. She fed and groomed the queen as she lay the next generation of workers, the nexus and life's blood of a superorganism. Despite what humans called her, she did not rule, as much a slave to the pheromone cloud as the least of her daughters.

Following the sun, she soared out and away from the hive, laughing in pure joy at the speed and grace of her new neurons, her ultraviolet-seeing eyes and delicate, hypersensitive olfactory antennae. A field of buckwheat drew much of her attention, but she suppressed it to the back of her distributed mind to gaze with fascination at the panoply of flowers scattered around the village. On Lake Street she drew pollen from bright purple Russian sage while a bevy of boys taunted a little girl out on her pink bicycle. In the supermarket parking lot she flitted between spirea while Jim Hanks loaded canned goods from his pockets into the driver's seat of his rusty farm truck. Behind the church she pulled paralytic nectar from a rhododendron, and caught her breath at a naked man writhing on the couch with a middle-aged blonde in red lingerie.

She knew those hands, firm but gentle as they gripped the pulpit, now buried in the deepest of perversions. She knew that black hair, short but unkempt, as a man of God had no need for frivolous vanities. She knew those lips, spewing filth where on Sundays they spoke of abstinence and righteousness.

She tried to flit closer, to catch a glimpse of the woman's face.

But the foragers darted among the flowers, drinking deep of the sweet, tingling liquid, and ignored her commands, her requests, her desires. Another fleeting pass by the window showed her a flash of gold—a wedding ring. Blonde, athletic but not too young, married; it could have been anyone.

Carr's Sunday voice thundered through her, each pronouncement a condemnation of sin and temptation, the "natural urges" sent by Lucifer to bring man to the level of dogs and then cast them out of the House Eternal to wallow in the cold and darkness outside of God's grace. His baritone had terrified her through her whole life, the promise of eternal damnation a weight on her soul as she tried dating, an ever-present judgment that thrust her into a gibbering panic the first and only time a boy had unbuttoned the top of her blouse, the Valentine's Dance six years earlier. His righteous fire consumed her in guilt when she touched herself, the only hands she'd ever felt.

Frustration bubbled as the foragers retreated, flowing back in waves to the colony as the sun went down. Her world closed in as the last of the field bees crawled inside, joining their brethren in quarters so cramped she couldn't move without brushing legs, body, or wings against her sisters. The foragers took no breaks, but instead fanned nectar to pull out the water and convert it to honey for the long cruel winter, filling the colony with an all-consuming buzz while the nurse bees fed and cared for the larvae as they had all day. Finally a part of something she understood, even so claustrophobia crushed Jamie's chest, buried her under infinite bodies, too close, far too close, a smothering darkness from which she might never escape. She struggled against the confinement, reaching desperately toward something, anything.

Gasping, Jamie bolted upright, eyes wide to take in the light of the quarter moon illuminating the small yard behind her trailer. Sucking in sweet air, she gulped down the taste of the night. Her body weighed her down, unable to fly, to spread itself throughout the town and become one with the bounties offered there. The sense of choking confinement shuddered through her, squeezed her throat shut, ravaged her bones and organs with utter desperation.

The iron grip softened and she focused on a lump in the grass. Earl Pruitt's smoker lay on its side next to the hive. Omnipresent crickets overwhelmed the buzz from the colony, joined by the high-pitched peeping of frogs from the unkempt pond across the street. Snatching up the smoker, she popped the lid to reveal nothing but cold ash.

It smudged her fingers, made them slippery. Holding it to her nose through her veil, she breathed in deep and smelled only char—

no exotic spice, no wax or vanilla, only the harsh incense of dark, pagan sacraments.

A desperate loneliness squeezed her heart. Her whole life she'd wanted something, something less stifling, some way to escape, something more to belong to. A taste of that smothering freedom had left her mouth dry in desperate anticipation to feel it again. Scrambling, she found enough small sticks and dried grass to fill the fire chamber, sparked a flame with her lighter, and pumped the bellows to build up a thick cloud of shimmering phantoms that glistened in the moonlight. She blasted the entrance, and the buzz lowered to a dull thrumming … but otherwise nothing happened.

She frowned, tried again, sucking smoke into her lungs as she did so.

Choking, chest burning, she rolled away from the cloud of guard bees that spilled from the entrance. They latched on to her bee suit, searching for a gap or thin spot to bury their stingers and die in defense of the hive, but found none. Stumbling to her feet, she walked toward the house, gently puffing smoke at the few guards that clung to her in order to maximize their deterrence, until at last they detached and fled home. Several bounced off her veil in a final warning before disappearing back toward the hive.

She stripped outside and left the suit on the railing in case of unseen stragglers caught in the folds, and hung the smoker on a plant hanger where it wouldn't cause a fire. Exhaustion dragged at her heels as she stumbled into the tiny kitchen, chewed numbly on a dinner she barely tasted, and crashed in bed. The clock glared an angry three a.m. Work started at seven.

She shuffled through the day, stocking clothes and bedding between helping customers. A blonde surveyed king sheets, middle-aged, a wedding ring on her finger. Jamie tried to remember if her hair had been that flaxen, if the calves beneath her knee-length skirt matched those wrapped around the preacher's thrusting backside. Would Carr's lover shop at the mall? Would Jamie recognize her if she did? Would Satan find her here, or find the preacher at his dalliances?

She couldn't be sure, and the dozen middle-aged blondes she

met through the day all could have been smiling with the secret knowledge of their carnal relationship.

After work, Jamie bustled home with an armload of groceries, gulped down a lukewarm TV dinner, and ducked out onto the stoop.

Earl Pruitt's smoker hung where she'd left it, the lone steel screw a shining beacon in the late afternoon sun. A curious worker bee hovered next to her gloves and hive tool, perhaps intrigued by the lingering signature of honey left behind in the ultraviolet spectrum. Her hands shook as she fired up the smoker, pumped the bellows to create a thick white cloud; it took three tries to zip up her suit, another two to secure her veil.

The hive rumbled as she approached, a sound her human brain interpreted as chaos, in reality the concerted dance of thousands of creatures dedicated to a singular, collective goal: survive the snows until dandelions bloom.

A whisper of smoke drifted across her vision, sweet ginger mingled with rich myrrh and charred pine. She blasted the entrance, and exploded outward into the fading day.

Jackson Bard screamed at his cowed wife next to their barbecue, a gold cross tangled in the thick hair springing from his white T-shirt. Light from the necklace sparkled off of a row of purple coneflowers, and the hemispheres atop the ring of purple gave a rich harvest of high-sugar nectar. Ankle-high chicory lined the roadside, low in nectar but loaded with pollen the same bright blue as its flowers that dotted the dirt shoulder next to Dave Cullen, handcuffed on his knees between his Camry and a police car, a half-empty bottle of ten-dollar whiskey spilled out at his feet. The alcohol and smoky resins drew her interest, but only for a brief moment. Late-season Dutch clover spotted the park lawn where Kylee Jones slapped the boy groping at her jeans next to a spilled picnic basket, each flower a bounty of sweet juice and bright white pollen.

She poured malice toward the boy who wouldn't take "No" for an answer, and envy erupted at Kylee for being young and attractive and charming and everything that Jamie couldn't seem to be. The young woman yelped and slapped at her neck.

Jamie cried out as she pulled away from the stinger embedded in the girl's skin, her guts tearing free in a streak of gelatinous goo to leave behind the venom sac, dismembered muscles still pumping venom into the wound.

A rush of pleasure brought her back to the coneflowers. Another three of her sisters died driving Bard from his wife and his meal, sending him stumbling for the safety of the indoors. She laughed, somehow without lungs or voice; the hive didn't mourn the loss, any more than a person mourns the hair or fingernails they discard on any given day.

The buckwheat distracted her, and she lost herself for a while in the snowy blossoms and the dark nectar, almost black with a taste like sweetened oatmeal. Regaining herself, she roamed the town from plant to plant, riding the cloud to the giant pink flowers of the rhododendron behind the church rectory, where the view into Pastor Carr's private sanctum should have found him preparing for the Saturday sermon the next day.

He sat at his desk, in full view of the highest bees, writing free-hand on loose leaf paper. Next to his pad sat a tangle as pink as the flowers, the thong's lace edge giving way to thin fabric meant for seduction, not practicality. He stroked it with a finger now and then, eyes closed, before going back to his work.

This man had denied her even thoughts of pleasure with his weekly promises of damnation and hellfire, all while he indulged his depravities at a whim, defiling another's marriage and his own vows for a taste sweeter than honey.

Her wrath meant nothing to the bees; behind the closed window he may as well have not existed. Snarling in frustration, she let her mind escape to the flowers, let it pull back into the hive with the setting sun, let it settle in turn to the business of evaporation and brood-rearing. As she came to on the ground, human once more, she grinned.

He'd be outside tomorrow. He had to drive to church.

Jamie slept in on Saturday, waking without the alarm at nine-fifty-two. She showered and ate lunch, bologna and American cheese on white bread, then read a little. With church at five, the pastor wouldn't leave his house until four. That gave her a few hours to clean house and do laundry, chores she'd neglected in favor of riding the cloud.

Sweaty, exhausted, but satisfied, she fired up the smoker and approached the hive at ten minutes to four. A puff, and she joined the swarm, consciousness spreading over the town to find her target.

Carr's Forrester wasn't in the driveway. Up, up she rode, into the whirling storm of drones and virgin queens, casting her gaze downward. He wasn't at church. Frantic, she scoured the streets, jumping from hedge to shrub to garden plot, until at last she found his dark green Forrester skulking in the shadows of a linden tree on Ringwood Circle.

She waited in the comfortable hum of the branches until Carr came outside. A peek through the doorway dashed her hopes of catching him in further depravity; a frail old woman held his hand as he left, letting go only when another step would have dragged her outside. Jamie wondered what she'd think of the panties he probably had in his pocket as he jingled his keys on the way to his car.

Fueled by Jamie's rage, her sisters rushed him, seeking out unprotected areas on his neck, face, and hands. She gritted her teeth as her guts came out, again and again, each sting a divine rebuke and a holy sacrifice that filled the air with the dense, banana-like scent of alarm pheromone.

Screaming and slapping at the already-dead bodies, he flung open the door and dove inside. Breathing hard, he stared wide-eyed out the window, apparently not knowing enough to scrape out the stingers before they could inject their full load of venom. She followed as he peeled away, his scowling face red with pain and anger. He sped, racing toward home or church at twenty over the limit, but not near enough to outrun the pheromone cloud that enveloped the town from her backyard.

A hollow filled her stomach, pulled and stretched like taffy, oozed as the stinger came out. One of her sisters had stayed behind, trapped in the preacher's clothes, violent and aggressive because of the scents her dying sisters had erupted all over his body. His car swerved as her body crushed between his hand and temple.

Jamie heard the crunch, and the cry, and the shrieks. From high in the air she saw the red streak stretching twenty feet behind and under Carr's vehicle, over the sidewalk and onto the lawn. Children gaped, horrified, at the mangled bicycle half-pinned under the Forrester's front grill.

She fled, up and away, riding the cloud to the buckwheat field, to the simplicity of sweet nectar and wholesome pollen, to a world where humans meant nothing and cars didn't crush little boys.

But when she woke, she cried, her sobs tearing out of her chest in the middle of the night, drowned by the symphony of crickets.

She went to the funeral, where a guest preacher presided, gently speaking of the evils of drink and speeding, and the power of compassion and forgiveness, and of a divine plan beyond our comprehension. He couldn't know that there had been no plan, only the petty envy of a sinful woman.

They shunned her, though from aggrieved apathy rather than malice. Surrounded by the people she'd called her own, she wallowed in the emptiness of their company. No one asked how she knew the boy, or why his death would bring her to such tears. No one pointed fingers, no one accused her. No one paid her any attention aside from the occasional curious glance.

No one except Mrs. Pruitt, who had as little place at the funeral as Jamie. Mrs. Pruitt stared at her through the service, and the internment, her rheumy eyes pinpoints of dark knowledge stabbing into Jamie's soul. She said nothing, though, only hobbled to her car to let a young man Jamie didn't know drive her home.

After, Jamie wept on her stoop, the world a blur of tears. Tires crunched on the gravel, drawing her gaze. An ancient minivan pulled into the driveway, "Pruitt's Bee Services" emblazoned on the side in fading yellow paint. The young man hopped out of the driver's seat, came around, and opened the passenger's side to let Mrs. Pruitt down, both still somber in their funeral attire.

She held his arm all the way up the walk, but when they reached the steps she stood tall and held out a gnarled hand.

"Give her back, dear. She doesn't belong to you."

Jamie scowled. "I bought it."

"She isn't *meant* for you, and I didn't come to argue. So stop dillydallying and give me the smoker."

The young man put sun-weathered fists on his hips, not quite relaxed, not quite threatening. He might have weighed two hundred pounds, too much of it lean muscle, and his scowl could break rocks.

Jamie reached under the step, pulled out the smoker, and froze, unable to let go. The farm boy snatched it from her grip and passed it to the old woman. Mrs. Pruitt sighed, eyelids fluttering, as she clutched it to her chest, lips upturned in a rapturous smile.

"You know what it can do?" Jamie asked.

Without opening her eyes, her lips turned down into a vicious snarl. "If you can't let it go it consumes you, and you die."

"Jesus," Jaime said.

"You have no idea, back before mites, before all the poisons. Today is a pale shadow of the past. We'd drift away for hours, Earl and I, sometimes for days, let the world crumble around us. That first winter was so, so hard. The second almost killed us." Her eyes snapped open, bored into Jamie, pupils reflecting nothing, not even the sunlight. "It took a long time to come back, to get used to human living again. Earl never did quite get the gist of it, God rest him. She's not something to give up lightly."

Jamie swallowed. "I get it. Even with … with everything that happened, everything that's wrong, I still want to do it again."

Mrs. Pruitt patted her hand, dry and firm, an unwelcome intrusion to her space and her body. "And you would, too, if I'd let you keep it. A moth to flame. No matter how much you tell yourself that young boy died because you played with something you shouldn't, that you wouldn't do it again, you would. Nobody's that strong, dear. You'd do it, knowing more terrible things would happen, and you'd feel bad and you'd do it again. And again." The old woman rolled the smoker around in her hands, face softening into almost fondness. "My husband's jealous mistress. She's been a thorn in my side a long time, and caused me more grief than is right. I tried to pull him away, one last time, and she killed him. Took his love and his faith and buried it under dry sod. But the farm isn't the same without her."

"Then why did you sell it—her?"

Pruitt grunted. "I didn't."

"You did. It was in—"

She stopped Jamie with an upraised hand, far too fast for her age. Her eyes crinkled as she smiled, but no light touched them. "Dearie, have you ever plugged up a hive to move it?"

Jamie swallowed. "Once, when I brought my first nuc home."

"And what did the bees do when you trapped them?"

"They tried to get out. Boiled out of a hole until I found and taped it up. Clawed at the screen. Stung the s— stuffing out of me when I got them home, too. I've never seen them so mad."

"That's right." Pruitt passed the smoker to her companion. "Like some people, honeybees don't like to be contained, and like some people, they seek to hurt those that contained them. I've kept her cooped up since Earl passed, and planned to do so until I join him. I guess she has other ideas."

"You can't destroy her."

Pruitt clucked her tongue. "Of course not."

"Then what? I mean, you're what, ninety-three?"

"Ninety-six." A hint of a smirk touched her lips. "Had a few years on Earl, even back then. I don't have much time, God willing, but I'll keep her from causing too much trouble from here out. It's best you don't know the details."

"But I need—"

"No. You want. And whatever it is you want, get it. Sell your home. Move to the city. Find yourself a man or a woman or a passion. But don't come back to the farm. It won't end well if you do."

Jamie sighed, stood, and tried not to stare in longing at the metal in the young man's hands.

"So that's it, then."

"That's it."

Mrs. Pruitt allowed Jamie to help her down the walk and into the van while the young man started the motor. A honeybee lay upside-down on her dashboard, unmoving, desiccated by the midday sun. She swept it out onto the road with her hand, said goodbye, and faced forward. Jamie closed the door and stepped back.

They drove out of sight. Moments later the dead bee quivered, stood, and took to the air, racing after her queen.

A CREATIVE URGE

Tears streamed down Cassie's face as she smeared paint across the canvas with her bare hands. Bilious green covered the pond in the foreground, smothered the silhouette of children on swing sets and the craggy, vine-covered trees clawing at the sky behind them, obliterating a month's work under its unrelenting stain. She dipped her hand into another can, and it came up dark red like old blood. That red mingled with green in vicious slashes to form a muddy brown, the same muddy brown that covered the torn and broken canvasses littering her studio floor.

The urge to destroy is also a creative urge.

Mikhail Bakunin's words gave her no succor as she tore the last of her portfolio from the easel and broke it across her knee, smearing herself with more paint, mangled colors that already covered her T-shirt, shorts, bare feet, and every inch of her skin. Chest heaving, sweaty paint dripping in her eyes from tangles of paint-soaked hair, she finally collapsed to a sitting position on the floor.

For a moment, all she could do was breathe, lightheaded, even hunger a memory of something some other her might feel.

Before the accident, her last four paintings—all fields of flowers—had sold for a combined total of twenty-eight thousand dollars, almost matching the salary she earned as a science teacher at a prestigious but chronically underfunded charter school. After the accident, her next three—still nature scenes, but dark and haunted—had sold for eighty thousand dollars. An up-and-coming hot property on the New York scene, she'd quit her job and rented a larger space, large enough to paint what she wished, when she wished. Somewhere she didn't have to share with roommates, and with a lover only if she wanted to.

She didn't want to.

It didn't make the slightest bit of sense that somebody could be there one moment and not be there the next, love and light and warmth replaced by a broken doll of cold meat and cracked bone. They'd caught the man that had killed Tess, convicted him of manslaughter on a suspended license after three DWIs, sentenced him to ten years in prison—ten years to pay for a lifetime—and it had done nothing to bring her back.

Life held no closure, only endings.

The ability to pinpoint the moment her mind had slipped didn't make Cassie feel any better. After the call, she'd insisted on seeing the body, barging past her unwilling and hostile mother-in-law to kiss those cold, bloody lips one last time, to slip the ring from her wife's finger and put it on her own, until death did them part. She'd grieved, and how she'd grieved, but hadn't broken. No, that came later.

During the trial she'd insisted on looking at the crime scene photographs, digital images of red blood on green grass where Steve Barrington's SUV had hit Tess at seventy miles an hour, throwing her mangled body from the sidewalk into the park. Cassie knew every curve of that body, had more than once peeled the sunshine yellow jogging suit from it, but in that misshapen mass she recognized none of her love.

And yet, a knife of familiarity stabbed behind her eye at the twisted lines and unnerving curves that had once been her Tessie's limbs. A body couldn't lie like that, not in a Euclidean world, not in a universe where colors were merely spectral frequencies interpreted by primates who'd outgrown the jungle, where shapes defined a three-dimensional space of real things. A body couldn't take that shape, and a mind couldn't see it, not without a slip, a fracture, a bending of what is to accommodate what had to become. Such a shape could not exist, not in human form, not in any form.

But it did, right there in full color, on glossy print too flat to encompass that terrible form. Cassie knew that shape with the deepest part of her being, and despite the months since, it would not let her go. The shape ate her dreams, turned every waking moment into a nightmare of need—to see it again, to never see it again, to think about it always and never. That moment, that glimpse of the picture before the detective had hidden it away, had stolen her capacity for joy and love, kidnapped her muse, and replaced both with a need she didn't understand.

The urge to create is also a destructive urge.

She stumbled into the pile of canvases, knocking them aside with her legs, and fell to her hands and knees. Scrabbling through them, she found a dry one she'd ruined days before, back when she still ate, before she'd run out of booze, before her phone had died and taken with it her link to the world outside her apartment. She wiped paint from her hands onto her shirt and picked it up, adding fingerprint smudges to the edge as she set it on the easel.

Streaks of red and green melded through the dark brown substrate, whorls and streaks that were, at least, possible whorls and streaks. Far too possible.

With a trembling hand, she picked up a brush, and a pot of canary yellow paint, almost the same color as her wife's jogging suit. She dipped the brush, and pulled back with a hiss. A bead of red blood formed across the inside of her thumb where she'd cut it on the lid. Another her, one from another life, she might have sucked the blood from the injury, applied a Band Aid, perhaps some antibiotic ointment. Instead, this her, the new her, the her who couldn't unsee that abominable shape, gripped the brush and let the blood run in rivulets down her forearm and across her fingers.

Tess's shattered body screamed through the void, guiding Cassie's hand as it slashed across the canvas, painting streaks and bends in too many dimensions to mimic the broken form her murderer had left on the grass. Cassie's blood trickled down the brush and spotted the canvas. She attacked it with the bristles, melding it with the yellow to create a cacophony of hues from deep ochre to bright sunshine and everything in-between. Layer built upon layer as the sun set in ambers and slept then rose blood red to the sounds of distant church-bells and set again under stars that blazed blue-white, until at last Cassie stumbled back and fell to her knees, eyes locked on the dark majesty of her creation.

The yellow glyph blazed from the canvas like the moon—no, as the moon—and somehow stretching up to and beyond that moon stood jagged spires that reached into an infinite midnight sky, a great crystalline city formed complete from whorls of dark red and green and brown. A city she had no memory of painting. In such a city, lovers could shatter into impossible tangles of flesh and bone yet live still to shed their moonlight, and under such moonlight could dark between-creatures raise their haunted voices in dissonant, piteous praise of a master that knew no pity.

In such a city a spouse could die yet become the moon.

Cassie reached forward as if to touch the moon that was her wife, and her eyes widened in wonder. Her fingers took on a pallid gleam not from the windows, not from the incandescent bulbs hanging from the ceiling, but from the moon-glyph's soft glow. She basked in her wife's cool mystery, arms dotted with goosepimples from the breeze off the lake.

A thought seized her, wonderful and terrible and inevitable.

Towers so tall they touch the moon.

Dark waters, before unseen and also unpainted, lapped at the cracked, rocky shores of the impossible city, yellow moonlight also flickering from those moving waves, Tessie-shimmers in an eternal, dappled dance. From that shore a faint breeze carried the taste of salt, and blood, and the faint, nose-wrinkling memories of dead fish and rotting seaweed.

With that breeze on her skin, the scent of the ancient shore in her lungs, she closed her eyes and crawled through.

Water, too hot and so, so cold, covered her hands and knees, lapped at her thighs and elbows, soaked her clothes and weighed her down. It caressed her, called to her, tugged gently at her sweatshirt, offered her sweet sleep under its glossy surface. But that surface reflected the moon. With murmured thanks for the offer, she shed her wet clothing and stepped onto the shore, let the wind bring goosebumps to her pale, paint-smeared skin. The water's cooed disappointment drowned under the lap of waves.

Jagged rocks pricked at her feet, cut them as she crossed the dark crystal shards, some as large as swords, most ground to fine sand. Wet footprints tinged red with smeared brushstrokes behind her as she approached the great, clutching spires, taller than the tallest of mountains, taller than the heavens. She turned from them to look up at the spires.

Taller than the moon. My moon.

Between-creatures carried their shadows with them as they slinked from building to building, watched her approach with chittering anticipation. She walked, and walked, for unknown hours, hours and days, as the curve of the earth revealed more and more of the city below the horizon. When at last she got close enough that the impossible city met the ground, the between-creatures sang to her shrill notes no human voice could sing, Riemann harmonies no human mind could hold dancing in prime numbered time-signatures, hard warnings and soft blessings in a language she didn't understand.

She hummed to them in her own rough way, too human, too real, and yet they heard her, and sniffed the air, and came to her. They offered their hands, as jagged and broken as the rocks that had shredded her calloused, scarred feet so long ago. Cloaked in shadow and tipped with shining black claws, their hard fingers dripped a silky venom that twinkled with unlight. She took those offered hands, ran her soft fingers across their roughness, touched her fingers to her tongue to taste their poison, bittersweet like honey and turpentine. It burned her throat, brought a rough edge to her song, and they sang it with her.

They took her hands again and led her forward, into the city, and then up, and up, always higher, toward that soft yellow light. Where there were stairs or ladders leading upward or bridges across the black chasms between spires she took them, and where there were not she made them, painting them with her mind in reds and greens and browns in her quest to reach the moon that was her love.

Bright blue stars birthed and died and birthed and died, born and reborn from the nuclear ashes of their ancestors, an endless ballet without rhyme or purpose casting metals through the void, to live and die in an endless dance of birth and death and heavier, explosive rebirth. Yet in those strange eons the sun never rose, never set, never dared show its face, never dared hide her love of the moon.

And the moon, her moon, never moved, never once yielded its place in the sky. Yellow paint dripped from it to spatter across the gantries and bridges and towers of the silent city, Tess's broken light swallowed by the darkness that could not be satiated even as it dripped across Cassie's bridges and staircases, even as it dribbled into the dark, hungry seas that surrounded the impossible city. But still the moon dripped, and never did its paint-light wane.

She climbed, and the between-things climbed with her, and as they climbed her body withered, skin stretched tight over bone and gristle and desiccated muscle, organs drying and crumbling to nothing, yet still full of glorious, unending purpose. It didn't matter—she could still walk, still paint, still climb.

And how she climbed.

The between-creatures sang to her their impossible songs while she climbed, and as the eons passed she learned them, joined their harmonies with her own, singing their song to the moon, her moon, her broken love, dripping its yellow light across broken spires and breaking waves. Again and again she reached for it with shadow-cloaked claws dripping silky black venom that twinkled with unlight, her straining voice keening with the need for one more touch, one more embrace, one more kiss of her lover's yellow light.

TAPS

Molly froze, her backpack half-in and half-out of her locker. It came again, a series of taps and scrapes behind the wall, a repeating rhythm that reminded her of the classic jazz drummers on her dad's old CDs, Billy Higgins and Jack DeJohnette, Art Blakey and Buddy Rich. The old guard who'd inspired her to pick up the sticks while her friends gravitated to the clarinet or the flute, the tomboys maybe braving the trumpet or sax.

For eleven years she'd played the drums, straight through to her junior year. She knew a great beat when she heard one. It sounded again, almost urgent, then cut off in a shriek of metal on metal.

"Hey!" Kirsten's voice cut through the rhythm like a scythe. The five-four brunette bounced on her heels and clutched her geometry book against a pale green sweater that matched her fingernails. "You're late for class."

"Speak for yourself." Molly pocketed her cell phone and produced a blue slip of paper. "I have a pass." She nudged her locker shut with her hip and hustled into step with Kirsten, the rhythm a memory hammering at the back of her mind.

"What did your mom say? About Saturday?" Kirsten's voice held too much hope, and Molly hated to crush it.

"She said, 'No.' And not the *maybe* kind of 'No.'"

"Did you tell her there wouldn't be any boys?"

Molly nodded. "Yeah, and she agreed. And no girls. Or animals. Or pizza delivery. 'Just because it's February Break doesn't mean you don't have work to do.'"

Kirsten stopped dead in front of Mrs. Bigg's room. "Oh, c'mon, how will she even find out from Atlanta?"

Shoving past, Molly ducked inside so that Kirsten couldn't see her eyes rolling. Even from her conference in Georgia, Molly's mom would learn of any transgressions against The Rules. She had neighbors checking in at all hours, a task force of busybodies with one relentless goal: ruin all fun.

Mrs. Bigg glanced their way long enough to notice the blue pass and then let them sit without interrupting her speech, something about congruent triangles and the stability of bridges. She sat next to Chris DeSouza and looked over his shoulder to copy the notes she'd missed.

In the back of the room the heater pinged and hissed, the metal cycling through hot and cold phases. As it expanded and contracted, the incessant shudder transitioned into the tapping rhythm from her locker, then back into random noise.

"Did you hear that?" she whispered.

Chris shook his head without taking his eyes from the smart board.

She tapped the rhythm on her desk. The heater answered, then they did it in unison.

"Miss Fitzgerald?" Mrs. Bigg's voice cut through her concentration, and the beat disappeared with it. "Can we keep the percussion in the band room?"

Molly cast her eyes down to her page. "Sorry, Mrs. Bigg."

Sounds followed Molly down the hallway to the drinking fountain: a rattle as the winter wind shrieked past the window, a jingle of keys in Principal Lawson's pocket, a subtle tapping down the lockers, each with the same distinct pattern. The hair stood on her arms, and an electric shiver coursed up her spine.

Kneeling to collect her *Anthology of American Literature*, she ran her fingertips across the thick white cover, then put her nail against the back of the locker and tapped, hard, repeating the pattern as she'd heard it.

Silence, not even her own breath, held in anticipation of a reply.

A hand grabbed her wrist, stark white and ice-cold. Molly shrieked and fell back. Her head rang and pain blasted the back of her skull, a black void filled with frozen stars, their cruel light reaching down to rob her of warmth and love and humanity.

Black tendrils wrapped her, squeezing and lifting her up into the darkness. She screamed again and tried to punch, kick, bite.

"Whoa!" Chris stumbled back, hands raised in a defensive posture, as the world slammed into place, too bright and too real.

"What … I …?"

With his face scrunched with worry, he knelt to pick up her fallen bag.

"You hit your head."

She rubbed her wrist, numb from the cold, and looked into her locker. Aside from her books and folders, it held nothing, with no room for a person or a void or stars. The *Anthology* sat undisturbed in the bottom.

"You okay?"

She dragged her eyes away from the book to look into his baby blues. "Yeah, I think so. Just a spider, freaked me out."

He scowled at her wrist. "I've never seen spider bites like that. Maybe you should go to the nurse. Get some cream or something."

She looked down at the string of hot, mottled-pink welts rising from her skin. They looked feverish, but felt like frostbite. "Yeah. Thanks."

He kept pace with her to the end of the hall, then turned left to go to history. She went to the bathroom, locked herself in a stall, and took deep, steady breaths to calm her racing heart.

Fifth period, Molly dumped her lunch in the garbage can—chicken nuggets and mashed potatoes with lumpy white gravy and a side of boiled broccoli—and headed for the band room, ears pricked for tapping sounds that didn't come. Mr. Stevens turned away from the shelf on the back wall, the one that hid the ugly metal access door between the practice rooms, and gave her a cursory wave on his way back to his desk.

She sat. The smooth sticks belonged in her hands, and her right foot found its home on the pedal to the love-worn bass drum.

A heavy beat rolled from the bass as her foot pumped. Twirling the sticks once, she set into the snare with a *piano* drum roll, building it up to a *forte* before launching into an improvised solo.

The rhythm flowed out of her, a fire in her arms and legs to defy the cold grip of … whatever the heck that was.

Sweat beaded on her forehead, so she switched tempo and brought it down to a dull roar.

The sticks writhed in her hands, and as she struggled to control them they hammered out a rhythm of their own, *the* rhythm, and cold dread shot through her bones. Her wrist throbbed in time. She forced an improvisation, but of their own volition her arms and hands flowed back to the driving beat. She looked up in alarm to see Mr. Stevens standing at the podium, arms crossed, a bemused look on his face.

She stopped with a crash on the high-hat, letting the discordant clang jar through her teeth like fingernails down a chalkboard.

"Where'd you get that groove?" A baby-faced twenty-something, his light brown goatee helped keep people from mistaking him for a student, but Molly always thought his gray eyes hid a weariness he never quite revealed.

Squirming under the scrutiny, she set the sticks down and met his eyes.

"Not sure. Why?"

He chuckled. "It's Morse Code. I did two years as Signals Intelligence in Qatar."

Everything in her screamed not to ask, but she had to. She licked her lips.

"What does it mean?"

He tapped it out on the podium. "F. I. N. D." He paused, then started again. "M. E. Period." He played it again and again, speeding up with every repetition, and the room shuddered in time. Eyes closed, he didn't seem to notice the shaking walls, the oppressive darkness as gray clouds swallowed the midday sun, the deep throbbing pulse of blood in her skull.

"STOP!" She pressed the heels of her hands to her ears to block out the sound.

His hands hovered above the podium, the smile frozen on his face. Sunlight streamed through the windows, blinding against the snow blanketing the hillside.

"How about this?"

He started again, a different pattern, longer.

She waited for him to finish before speaking.

"What did that say?"

"It said, 'Codes are for hiding things.'" Slumping to rest his chin on the back of his hands, he glanced at the clock—twenty-two minutes to the bell—and scowled. "Where'd you say you heard that?"

She shrugged. "I don't know. Just sort of came to me."

"Hell—um, heck of a coincidence, getting every letter. Even the punctuation"

"Yeah, that's really weird. Maybe it came from one of my dad's movies or something and has been bouncing around in my head."

"War movies?"

Nodding, she picked up the sticks and stood. "Yup. Vietnam and World War Two, mostly. He loves the old classics, and documentaries."

Mr. Stevens grimaced. "Never saw the real thing, did he?"

She shook her head. "No. Grandpa served in Korea, though. Mom's dad, too."

"I thought as much." Eyes raised to the clock, he clucked his tongue. "Time flies, and I've got work to do. Feel free to play until the bell."

"Thanks, Mr. Stevens."

He walked back to his desk and picked up a stack of sheet music off his chair, then sat.

FIND ME. The words flashed through her mind as she picked

up the mallets and turned toward the xylophone. FIND ME. She shivered, closed her eyes, and launched into a cover of Copa Cabana, upbeat and airy and not at all dark and cold.

Behind her the wind rattled the window, and she understood what it said.

FIND ME.

Molly opened a math book on her dresser, turned up the volume on her iPod, and ignored both in favor of her laptop. Fingers soft on the keys, she typed in, "Morse Code Translator" and hit "Enter."

She tried a phrase, listened to it, tapped it out on the bedframe, over and over to commit it to memory. Then another phrase, and another.

An hour later she fell back, head on the pillow, and stared up at the white ceiling, tracing routes through the uneven glossy patches. Beads of sweat cooled on her forehead, and she breathed hard as the songs faded into memory.

No. Not songs. *Messages.*

The next morning, Kirsten met her as she got off the bus. "How you feeling?"

Molly shrugged. "What do you mean?"

"Chris said you hit your head pretty good yesterday, and I didn't see you at all after. Figured you went home."

They meandered toward homeroom on scuffed, faded tiles. Lockers jiggled, shoes shuffled across the floor. Heating vents flooded the hall with tepid air. Molly pricked her ears at every sound, but in the cacophony of human voices she couldn't pick out any patterns.

Fingernails dug into her shoulder.

"Ow!" She flinched back and gave Kirsten a wounded look. "What the heck?"

Kirsten let go and let out a theatric sigh. "What planet are you on? Have you heard a single thing I've said?"

Shaking her head, Molly tried a sheepish grin. "Sorry? Just a little distracted, I guess."

Kirsten rolled her eyes. "Yeah, well, don't be rude."

They walked in together, said the Pledge of Allegiance after the bell, and suffered through thirty minutes of group work with Chad and Tom, the least mature boys in the history of ever. Their constant, childish snickering tore through Molly's head until she just couldn't take another moment. Her hand shot up.

"Yes?" Mr. Brown raised his eyebrows but didn't look up from his newspaper.

"Can—may I go to the bathroom?"

He looked up at the four of them, a dubious frown dragging on his expression. "Are you done?"

"It's an emergency."

She ignored Tom's chuckle and hurried to the door the moment Mr. Brown nodded.

Alone in the hall, she walked toward the bathroom but stopped at the first locker. Reaching out with one fingernail, she tapped a pattern. WHERE ARE YOU?

Nothing happened. She laughed.

What'd you expect, Mol? You're just going crazy.

She took two steps, and at the end of the hall a door opened with a scattershot creak more dots than dashes. A little seventh grader, wide-eyed in glasses way too big for his face, stepped out and walked her way. The door squealed closed with the same rhythm as the kid disappeared around the corner.

Looking both ways, she pulled out her phone and put the pattern into the translator. Goosebumps crawled up her arms as the temperature dropped ten degrees. Something scraped against the inside of the locker, mouse-feet rustling almost too quiet to hear.

BENEATH

Molly reached back, hesitated, then repeated the word with her fingertip, adding a question-mark. BENEATH?

Another pattern. She plugged it into her phone as humid air condensed on the screen.

SO COLD

Teeth chattering, she tapped, combining the new word with one she'd memorized. BENEATH WHERE? Her breath billowed in white clouds as she waited for a reply.

SO COLD

The temperature dropped again, and ice crystals crept across the windows.

The kid with the huge glasses rounded the corner, staring at her with wide eyes. She let out a breath she hadn't realized she'd been holding. "What, kid?"

His eyes frosted over, a cataract of ice crystals. She stumbled back and he grabbed her wrist, his touch icy daggers ravaging her skin straight through her sweater. The chittering noise that came from his mouth belonged to a world of shattered glass and pain and rocks cracking under the force of new-formed ice.

She jerked away and ran. Locker doors thundered an unrelenting staccato FIND ME as she ran past. Windows and door locks rattled FIND ME. The air in the vents whispered underneath and around the maelstrom of noise, repeating the boy's words in time with her throbbing wrist. Clutching it against her chest, the hall blurred through a sheen of tears.

She busted into the bathroom, shut herself in a stall and huddled there. Squeezing her hands over her ears, in a desperate attempt to make it stop, did nothing. Even the dripping of the fountains pressed their command. FIND ME.

She closed her eyes and replayed the boy's message in her mind. Hands shaking, she brought up the translator and fed the pattern into the phone.

I HEAR YOU PLAY

Noise flooded the room, human noise, girls chatting and arguing, classes changing in the hall. She let out a relieved sigh and opened the stall, joining the typical press of girls trying to freshen up in their allotted four minutes. She washed her hands, wincing as her sweater rubbed raw on her wrist, and ducked out into the hallway without speaking to anyone.

Heart thundering, Molly hurried past the janitor's cart, muffling the keys' jingle with her hand, praying nobody heard in the din of students grabbing last-minute things from their lockers and heading for the buses. She slipped the keys into her coat pocket, the metal cold against her shaking fingers, too cold, like the janitor had just been outside.

Principal Lawson returned her tight-lipped smile with pearly teeth and a hearty, "Have a good weekend!"

The kid's message rang in her ears. Where could you hear her play, behind foam-covered walls and thick, noise-isolating doors? What hidden place held those answers? Only one.

She shuffled toward the exit then cut right, through the internal fire doors and around the corner to the band room. After a soft knock, she pushed her way through.

"Hello? Mr. Stevens?"

With no answer, she pulled her practice sheets from her cubby, a tiny space for music and spare sticks dwarfed by those for the saxophones, trombones, and tubas. She stuffed the loose papers into the bottom of her bag, under her textbooks and folders. That done, she walked over to Mr. Stevens's desk, grabbed a sheet of paper from the printer, and opened the top drawer for a pen.

A silver oval caught her eye, the dull metal held by a beaded chain. She picked it up and read the dog tags. MARTIN, JAMIE E. The letters scraped their way through the shelf in the back of the room as she read them; she didn't have to look them up, didn't have to translate them.

Hands trembling, she took a picture, put them back, and wrote a quick note.

Mr. Stevens,

I lost my practice music.
Can I get another copy on Monday, please?

Thanks,
Mol

She closed her eyes, took a deep breath, and turned toward the far wall. Between the two practice room doors a black metal shelf held a legion of dusty trophies dating back sixty years. From tarnished brass to cheap plastic, they chronicled the victories of every competition and ignored the countless others where they found only defeat. She slid the shelf to the side, legs screeching against the floor to reveal the portal behind.

Marked AUTHORIZED PERSONNEL ONLY in bold red letters, the peeling paint gave her an indication of how often anyone used it.

She pulled the ring of keys from her coat, the jingles spelling out HERE HERE HERE as she searched for the one that matched the number on the lock.

Her fingers blistered as frost rimed the metal, and she shivered in her coat at the bitter cold. Jamming the key into the lock, she hissed against the pain and turned it. A jerk, a sigh of freezing cold air, and darkness yawned in front of her.

A steel ladder descended into a square hole in the concrete floor, the bright yellow paint faded from years of neglect. Black mold smudged the walls with angry splotches. Breath frosting, she pulled out her phone and used the flashlight app to blast the bright white LED down the hole.

Molly gasped.

A skeletal hand rested against the bottom rung. Beside it lay a caved-in skull on patchy gravel. She rubbed her wrist and frowned at the rusty handcuffs linking the arm to the unyielding metal. The body wore the tattered remnants of a uniform, dull gray-and-white camouflage just visible in the mold and rot. Her eyes grew wide as the finger twitched, the signal ringing out on the metal.

RUN

She stumbled back and slammed the door, groping for the keys. The ring fell from her fingers and clattered to the floor. She knelt to pick them up but instead grabbed the shelf and jerked it back into place. A trophy tottered as the band room door opened. She caught it and set it down next to the blazing heater. Suddenly too hot she swooned, light-headed. Pushing the keys under the shelf with her foot, she stood.

Mr. Stevens raised his eyebrows at her, the exact look he gave anyone late to class, or goofing off instead of playing. "Looking for something, Miss Fitzgerald?"

She swallowed, and tried not to gasp in a breath, instead pulling it slowly through her smile. "Hi, Mr. Stevens. I can't find my practice music. Was just leaving you a note."

He pulled the cart loaded with music stands the rest of the way into the room, let the double-doors close, then pushed it against them. Wiping his hands on his shirt, he walked forward. "From the floor?"

A nervous giggle escaped her lips. "No. My shoelace came untied. The note's on your desk."

He glanced at it, picked up the pen, clicked it a couple times. "From my drawer?"

She shrugged. "I didn't have one."

"You saw the dog tags, then."

"Dog tags?" Playing dumb never came easy to her, and he didn't look convinced.

He took another step, picked up the trophy, and then leaned in too close. Staring down at her, he licked his lips. "You're not special. She talks to me, too, you know."

She met his eyes, blank brown orbs, flat under the fluorescent light. "What?"

He brushed his knuckles across her cheek, then settled the hand on her shoulder and tapped, his fingernail sharp against her neck. He spoke the words as they seared across her nerves. "I. Loved. You." His grip tightened on her shoulder, twisting her coat until it pulled tight under her arm. "She looked like you, a little. I mean, not anymore."

Molly screamed. He swung the trophy and the world exploded in hot white light. Pulling herself from the floor and unsure how she got there, her eyes came to focus on the line of red drool hanging from her lips. Searing pain shocked through her chest as his shoe impacted her ribs, again and again. He dragged her to her tiptoes, her scalp on fire, one hand tangled in her hair, the other still holding the bloody trophy.

Feet dangling, legs useless, she tried to reach him, tried to claw or hit, tried to scream through the iron tang of blood in her mouth.

"No one can hear you, Molly, not through these walls."

She knew it. The sound-proofing and thick wooden doors did more than prevent dead spots. Words came, thick and hard to understand around her swollen tongue.

"Please, Mr. Stevens. I don't know—"

His face twitched, a spasm gone as fast as it came. "Don't play dumb. You're smarter than that, and it's … it's insulting. Jamie insulted me, near the end, after all we had and all we went through. She said she loved me, lived for me, but didn't show it, not after a while. Little niggling, nagging, grating insults, day in and day out. That's not love." He shoved her backward without letting go and she tried to protest around her fat lip. A tooth shifted and a jolt of pain shot up her jaw.

"Please, Mr. Stevens. Please, don't."

"Too late for that. She talked to you, you listened. You think you're the first? You're not. You're not special. You're not first. Just the first to find her. Maybe she wants company."

He pulled a handful of pills from his coat, pried open her mouth, and stuffed them in, jamming his fingers past her bite, forcing them to the back of her tongue. Tilting her chin up, he plugged her nose and rubbed her throat. She tried not to swallow, but swallowed. He held her against the wall, cruel hands crushing into her neck, until the world swam and her tongue grew thick in her mouth. A cloud bore her to the ground.

Dark eyes stared down at her. "Goodbye, Molly."

Cold. Too cold to shiver, too cold to breathe. She reached out in the darkness for something, anything to hold on to. Her fingertips brushed something smooth. She stretched, reaching, and pulled the orb toward her. It scraped across the floor in the pitch black, and a tear escaped as her fingers traced over the top to the brow, eye sockets, empty nasal cavity, and ruined teeth.

February break. Friday afternoon through the following Monday morning.

Ten days, give or take. Ten days before anyone would look for her in school, and no one to miss her at home. Ten days in the frigid dark, with black mold and Jamie Martin's skeleton for company.

She couldn't feel her toes, and her ankles burned through her socks.

The skeleton next to her shifted, a faint rustle almost too quiet to hear. Its finger rang against the ladder, staccato taps she couldn't put together without the translator. Molly reached for her phone, thrust her fingers deep into empty pockets, and let out a sob.

Frigid air slithered through her lungs, stagnant and precious proof of life.

Jagged shards of white-hot agony shredded her chest as she tried to lift herself from the ground. She collapsed next to the skull, panting. She'd broken her leg in Pee-Wee soccer a long time ago. This felt like that, only all over.

Cheek against the ice-cold floor, she reached out one-handed, feeling in the dark for anything that might help her. Brittle clothing crumbled at her touch, revealing naked bone beneath, jagged and splintered where Jamie's ribs had fractured. An old belt, stiff in the cold, the metal buckle frozen to the floor, but no bags, no tools, no walkie-talkie or phone or radio.

She moved higher, tracing the outstretched arm over the handcuffs to the twitching hand, tapping away a fervent message too fast and too long for her to understand. It calmed as her hand covered it, and it tapped a single word.

WARM

She tried to speak, but no sound escaped her ravaged throat. Instead she slid her index finger past and tapped a memorized phrase on the ladder. WHO ARE YOU

Images flooded her mind, a young woman in an Air Force uniform, short red hair and a beautiful smile. A helicopter ride over the desert. Mr. Stevens in uniform, on his knees, holding an open box with a gold ring inside. Fighting. Broken bones, a shattered jaw. Wounds hidden from family and friends back home.

Warmth and sorrow slithered into her, a life wasted and dumped in the eternal cold, seeking release. Seeking justice. Comfort.

Warmth. With the memories came patterns she hadn't had enough time to learn, the dots and dashes like second nature to a Signals Intelligence officer.

She tapped on Jamie's shattered skull. HOW DO WE GET OUT?

The skeletal hand tapped on the rung.

FIND ME

Molly joined her, and they tapped together.

FIND ME

Again and again in the dark, desperate, until hope faded and the cold took her and plunged her into hard, unrelenting nothing.

Molly woke in the darkness, alone and too warm, unnaturally warm. Her skin burned, liked chapped lips from too much skiing, but everywhere and nowhere, a disembodied pain that encompassed her entire world. Pushing through the agony, she felt but couldn't see her breath frosting against the back of Jamie's skull, the dead girl silent for the time being.

"I'm f-freezing. Can you—can you h-help me?" A piteous voice rasped from her throat, sore like poisoned needles in the back of her mouth.

The skeleton made no reply.

Jamie repeated the phrase.

Its finger twitched under her palm, lifted to the rung, and tapped.

HELP ME

"Yes. C-can you? Help me?"

HELP ME

"No, you don't understand. I n-need you to help me. I need to get out." The last phrase faded to nothing as her voice failed, throat too damaged to continue.

Jamie tapped.

GET OUT HELP ME HELP ME HELP ME GET OUT

Molly groaned and tried to stand. Her body protested, every motion a new study in just how much damage Mr. Stevens had done. She couldn't move her legs enough to sit, even pushing against the wall. She couldn't lift her arms enough to push up, and even trying sent spasms through her body.

Tears froze in her eyes. Words formed on her lips, too quiet for even the dead to hear. "You brought me here to die with you."

WITH YOU

WARM

WITH YOU

She closed her eyes, and slept.

"Hello?" A man, somewhere above, muffled and too quiet.

Frost crusted her eyelids, held them shut. She couldn't move, not even to lick her lips, as the voice called again.

"Molly Fitzgerald, you in here?"

Voices bantered back and forth, strong male voices, Principal Lawson and others she didn't recognize.

"She has to be. Cameras show she came in here, never came out."

"—her necklace in his car. We took him down to—"

"—nothing here."

"Maybe she—"

She tried to scream, to make any noise, but nothing came out. She tried to reach for the rung, but her hand didn't move. Her lips moved against the ice-cold skull, a desperate plea with her last shred of energy, movement without sound. "Help me."

A faint rustle and the skeleton shifted. Then bone rang on metal with sharp peals.

HELP ME

HELP ME

HELP ME

A voice above responded. "Do you hear that?"

"Morse code?"

Jamie tapped on, repeating the phrase again and again while Molly lay still, broken and unable to move.

"Is that a door?"

"Help me move this thing."

She tried to open her eyes, hold them open long enough to see the light, but the tapping faded and she knew no more.

The screaming wouldn't end. High, then low, then high, it shook her body and threw her side to side. She only knew pain, and unending screams. It hurt to move, it hurt to lie still. It hurt to breathe.

But she breathed, sweet country air tinged with bleach and the acrid bite of medicine.

I'm alive.

"She's waking up." A male voice, soft but urgent.

"Good. They'll want her statement at the hospital, if she's up for it."

Divine light blinded her, white and pure, and the shrieking faded to an ambulance's unsteady wail.

"Molly, can you hear me?"

"Yes." No sound came out of her raw throat. She tried again, and again, and squeezed her eyes shut against unbidden tears, hot on her skin. He shushed her.

"You're going to be okay. You've got some frostbite and hypothermia, a lot of broken bones, but we're keeping you warm and giving you fluids. They say you know Morse code. Can you tell us what happened?"

She reached out and he took her hand. Molly didn't know Morse code, no more than a few phrases. But Jamie did. Tracing her fingernail to his palm, they tapped.

ABOUT THE AUTHOR

Patrick Freivald is a four-time Bram Stoker Award® nominated author, a high school teacher (physics, robotics, American Sign Language), and a beekeeper specializing in hot pepper infused honey. He lives in Western New York with his beautiful wife, three parrots, two dogs, too many cats, and several million stinging insects—he's always had a soft spot for slavering monsters of all kinds.

He is the author of six novels and dozens of short stories, from hyper-violent kickass thrillers and teen zombie melodramas, to science fiction and horror and fantasy. Find him at Patrick.Freivald.com, on Facebook, Instagram, Twitter, and at www.FrogsPointHoney.com.

OTHER TITLES BY PATRICK FREIVALD

THE ANI ROMERO BOOKS:

Twice Shy
Special Dead

THE MATT ROWLEY SERIES:

Jade Sky
Black Tide
Jade Gods

WITH PHILIP FREIVALD:

Blood List

52451324R00134

Made in the USA
Lexington, KY
20 September 2019